THE GHOULS TAKE GREEN BAY

Blinded by the blood in his eyes, the farmer released the Warrior to wipe his left forearm across his face.

And Yama pounced, his right hand held in the Nukite position, and speared a piercing hand strike at the thing's throat, his training compelling him to go for one of the softest and most vulnerable areas on the human body. He felt his fingers sink into the yielding flesh halfway to his knuckles. Without missing a beat, as he drew his right hand back, he whipped his left hand in a Tegatana-naka-uchi, a handsword cross-body chop, connecting on the side of his opponent's neck.

Standing a few feet away, Melissa Vail heard a distinct snap and saw the thing go abruptly limp. "You did it!" she exclaimed in amazement.

The Warrior straightened, his eyes narrowing, "I was lucky."

"You were magnificent," Melissa breathed, her eyes sparkling, her cheeks flushed. "No one has ever broken their hold before. Usually, once one of those things grabs you, it's all over."

"I've never seen anyone behave the way this man did," Yama commented, moving to retrieve the Wilkinson. "It's as if he wasn't responsible for his actions, as if he was a robot."

"Now you know why we call their kind the walking dead."

Other books in the *Endworld* series:

ENDWORLD

#22:
GREEN BAY RUN

DAVID ROBBINS

LEISURE BOOKS ◼ NEW YORK CITY

Dedicated to Judy, Joshua, and Shane
We're back on track.

A LEISURE BOOK®

July 1990

Published by

Dorchester Publishing Co., Inc.
276 Fifth Avenue
New York, NY 10001

Copyright ©1990 by David L. Robbins

Printed in the United States of America.

Prologue

The wolves would feast on his corpse soon.

He reached the top of a low hill and glanced over his right shoulder at the pack of seven dark forms flitting through the forest. A shudder rippled along his spine at the thought of their glistening teeth crunching into his body. He gazed up at the afternoon sun, sweat caking his skin, then hastened down the hill.

How much farther?

After coming so very, very far, after traveling hundreds of miles and having survived encounters with scavengers, mutations, and wild beasts, the idea that he might die brought tears of frustration to the corners of his brown eyes.

Not now!

Not when he might be close to his goal!

His weariness caused him to stumble over a limb lying on the ground in his path. He maintained his balance with an effort and forged ahead, his hands gripping his Winchester tightly, his knuckles white.

One bullet.

All he had left was one lousy bullet!

If worse came to worst, if he continued to weaken and the wolves made their move, he could always use the last bullet on himself. At least he wouldn't be eaten alive. The horror of dying alone, lost somewhere in the wilderness of northwestern Minnesota, weighed heavily on his heart. The fact that he had failed his loved ones, that a terrible fate would befall them—if it hadn't already—contributed to his melancholy.

If only he could find the Home!

He surveyed the dense woods ringing him on all sides and frowned. Three weeks ago when he had departed Green Bay on his prized mare, locating the Home had seemed feasible. Now, he felt as if he were looking for the proverbial needle in a haystack. How could he hope to contact the Family without the exact location of their compound? He'd known the odds were against him when he started on his mercy mission, but he'd always entertained the optimistic belief that he would succeed despite the odds.

He had to succeed.

If he didn't, his wife and daughter were doomed.

A throaty growl sounded to his rear.

Startled, he spun and spotted a large gray wolf less than 15 feet away, standing there and regarding him intently.

"Beat it!" he shouted, thinking the sound of his voice might drive the animal off. "Go eat a rabbit!"

The wolf simply stood there, its black nose twitching, seemingly unaffected by the blistering August heat despite its heavy grizzled gray coat and long, bushy tail.

"Leave me alone!" he bellowed. He took a step toward the wolf and swung his rifle by the barrel. "Go!"

With an air of calm indifference, the wolf turned and padded softly into the undergrowth. In seconds the vegetation closed around its streamlined form.

But where were the others?

Were they preparing to attack?

He turned and resumed his trek to the northwest, ignoring the hunger pains in his stomach. When was the last time he'd eaten? Two days ago? Three? He shook his head, deciding his appetite didn't matter. He couldn't afford to stop to eat with the wolves on his trail. Even if the wolves quit their tireless, stealthy shadowing, he was reluctant to use his sole remaining bullet on game.

Now what had he been thinking about before the wolf interrupted him?

Oh, yes.

The Home.

His brow knit as he tried to remember every fact he had ever been told about the Home and the Family. A survivalist guy had constructed the 30-acre retreat before World War Three. Since the damn war had transpired 106 years ago, the Home's continued existence testified to the tenacity of its occupants, descendants of the survivalist and those he had selected to join him at the compound prior to the launching of the missiles.

Think.

What else did he know?

The Home, so the story went, was located in an isolated area not all that far from the Canadian border, on the outskirts of the former Lake Bronson State Park. According to the map he'd lost when his horse was killed, the Home must be north of State Highway 11 and east of U.S. Highway 59. He'd crossed over State Highway 11 an hour and a half ago, so if his calculations were correct, and if the whole tale about the Home wasn't a blatant Technic lie, then he must be close.

What if the story *was* a lie? he asked himself.

If so, he'd come all this way for nothing.

He shook his head, his lips compressing in a thin line, and resolved to quit being so negative. Sure, the story had sounded farfetched when he'd first heard a version of it from that drunken sot at the tavern he frequented on the outskirts of Green Bay. But then others had related similar accounts, and despite his better judgment he'd gradually accepted the reports as accurate.

Imagine!

Someone had actually beaten the Technics at their own ruthless game!

The various accounts all agreed on certain basic points. As always, the treacherous Technics had been up to no good. They'd learned about the existence of the Home and had deviously endeavored to extract an important secret from the Family. The exact nature of the secret was a mystery, but in light of the Technics' well-known interest in expanding the area under their control, it must have been important to their war preparations. The Family, somehow, had thwarted the Technics. Not only that, a Warrior from the Home had slain the Technic leader and thrown Technic City into turmoil. Once called Chicago, the metropolis was now enclosed within an electrified fence and the people were forced to abide by the autocratic dictates of their technocratic masters.

Thank God he didn't live in Technic City!

He would rather live on his small farm, rather have to contend with the uncertainties of rural life, than reside in a city where the people were subservient to technology, where machines mattered more than the persons running them. On the farm, at least, he enjoyed genuine freedom.

A raspy snarl came from the right.

Leveling the Winchester, he turned and saw two wolves watching him. They were growing bolder and bolder as the minutes passed. How long before they tried to bring him down? He realized they were probably as hungry as he was, otherwise they wouldn't be stalking him. Wolves seldom went after humans unless empty bellies prompted them to disregard their customary caution where homo sapiens were concerned.

A yelp sounded to the left.

He looked, and the skin on his back tingled when he saw two more wolves near a thicket. Incipient panic welled within him, but he swallowed hard, wheeled, and hastened to the northwest. Maybe the wolves would leave him alone for a while longer. Maybe they would wait for nightfall. Maybe he could hold them off if he climbed a tree.

Maybe. Maybe. Maybe.

A narrow stream materialized several dozen yards ahead, a ribbon of water flowing from north to south.

He increased his pace, licking his dry lips, eager to taste the cool liquid. If only he hadn't lost his canteen and all of his provisions when that band of scavengers shot his mare out from under him a week ago! Since then, he'd subsisted on whatever he could shoot for food, and he had been lucky enough to find a spring or a creek every other day or so to quench his thirst. Right at the moment his throat was parched.

A lone wolf appeared on the far side of the stream.

He halted and raised the Winchester to his right shoulder. If the wolves thought they were going to keep him from the water, they had another thing coming. He'd use his last bullet, if necessary, to slake his thirst.

The wolf, a huge beast sporting a white streak down its tail, walked to the water and began lapping greedily, its eyes on the man.

So the heat was getting to them, as well. He grinned and waited until the wolf finished and retreated into the brush, then he hurried to the water and dropped on his hands and knees. His craving made him careless. Without considering his safety, he set the rifle on the grass to his left and plunged his hands into the stream.

How refreshing the slowly flowing water felt on his fingers!

He laughed and leaned down to splash his face and neck, savoring the relief, feeling the liquid trickle under his tattered blue T-shirt and down his chest. The stream was four feet wide from bank to bank and half again as deep. Pebbles and loose gravel were on the bottom.

What if there were fish?

He lowered his mouth to the stream and sipped, knowing he might become sick if he drank too fast. Oblivious to all else, he swallowed and stared at his reflection on the surface. His unkempt black hair stuck out at all angles. The water distorted his hooked nose, giving him a birdlike aspect enhanced by his scarecrow frame. He looked down at himself, at his ragged jeans, estimating he had lost 20 pounds on the journey.

At that moment, when he was totally distracted, the patter of rushing feet arose behind him.

He tried to grab his rifle and straighten, but his pervasive fatigue hampered his reflexes. His left hand wrapped around the Winchester barrel, and then a heavy form crashed into his right hip and drove him forward.

Into the stream.

Water enveloped him, and under any other circumstances he would have welcomed the sensation, but now he was fighting for his life against a pack of feral foes who wanted his flesh to fill their stomachs. Sharp teeth tore into his right side. If he hadn't been underwater, he would have screamed. Instead, he flung his legs and right arm down, checking his descent, and surged erect, gasping for air when he broke the surface.

On his right a wolf snapped furiously at him while striving to secure a foothold.

He lifted the rifle, both hands on the barrel, intending to club the beast in the head, when a second wolf materialized on the west bank and crouched to spring. His arms whipped the Winchester in a downward arc and the stock caught the animal on the head, smashing into the wolf above the right eye and flinging the beast against the bank.

The second wolf scrambled to right itself, but its rear legs kept slipping on the side of the stream.

He took several strides to the south, backing away from both wolves, then darted to the west bank and clambered from the water. An adrenaline rush had supplanted his fatigue with a burst of energy, and he took advantage of his newfound vigor, shoving to his feet and fleeing to the northwest before either wolf could climb out. They would be on his trail in seconds, but he had a greater worry.

Where were the other five?

All day there had been seven wolves hounding him. He scanned the forest for them as he ran, his heart thumping in his chest. Would they leap from concealment or chase him, wear him down as they invariably did with deer and elk? Wolves customarily dogged a herd or individual victim, waiting for their quarry to exhibit any sign of weakness. They were Nature's gleaners. Their purpose in the natural order of things was to eliminate the sick, injured, and defective specimens they came across. A healthy deer, elk, or moose had nothing to fear from a wolf pack.

A short bark came from the south.

He looked over his left shoulder and gulped at the sight of a pair of wolves loping after him. They were deliberately holding back, running just fast enough to keep him in view.

The bastards!

His legs pumped strenuously as he weaved through a stand of saplings and reached a wide field. On the far side, at the north edge, reared a towering oak tree.

Salvation!

He made for the tree, confident he could resist the pack once he climbed beyond their grasp. An intense pain racked his right side where the wolf had bitten him. He knew he was bleeding, but he couldn't afford to take even a second to examine the wound. He singlemindedly focused on the oak to the exclusion of all else. A quick check to his rear brought goose bumps to his skin.

There were four wolves now.

And they were ever so slowly narrowing the gap.

No!

He breathed in great gasps as he sprinted toward the tree. A smile curled his mouth upward when he saw there were two low-hanging limbs he could use to vault to a safe perch. The wolves could howl and growl all they wanted, but he would be safe.

Or so he thought.

Until three wolves ran from behind the tree and fanned out in front of the trunk.

Stunned, he slowed and hefted the Winchester, uncertain of what to do. They had him cut off and hemmed in, at their mercy, and wolves weren't notorious for their compassion.

The trio near the tree had halted and were waiting for him, their mouths hanging open, their large, tapered canines and red tongues visible.

He stopped 20 feet from them and turned sideways so he could see both groups. The four pursuing him likewise stopped and gazed at his wheezing form. He aimed at one of the wolves to the north, then at one to the south, debating whether to shoot one in the hope the rest would take off.

A wolf to the north suddenly crouched, then charged straight at him.

Acting more on instinct than conscious design, he twisted, sighted, and squeezed the trigger. The booming retort and the bullet striking the ground inches from the wolf caused the beast to veer to the west and run several yards. He lowered the rifle and frowned in exasperation. He'd missed! His life was on the line and he'd missed!

None of the wolves had fled.

He reversed his grip and grasped the barrel, prepared to go down fighting.

One of the wolves to the south launched itself forward, hurtling at the human's legs.

Scarcely breathing, he elevated the stock and swung with all of his strength. The wolf easily evaded the blow, darting to the right and bounding beyond his reach.

Were they toying with him?

Several of the pack sat on their haunches.

Bewildered by their behavior, he scrutinized them, glancing from wolf to wolf, waiting for the first one to come at him. But they stayed where they were, staring, always staring, and if he didn't know better he would have sworn they were grinning at him, mocking him, well aware that all they had to do was bide their time and he would weaken enough for them to finish him off at their leisure. He looked at the tree, thinking he might try to break through them, and his eyes widened in astonishment when he saw a man standing less than a dozen yards to the left of the oak.

The newcomer wore a one-piece, seamless, dark blue uniform that fit snugly on his immense physique. His eyes were a penetrating blue, his short hair and sweeping mustache both an unusual silver shade. Over his left shoulder was slung a carbine. A revolver rested in a brown leather holster under his left arm, an auto pistol in a similar holster under his right. On his left hip rode a curved scimitar in a scabbard, and on his right a survival knife. "Hello," this walking arsenal said. "My name is Yama. Can you use some assistance?"

The wolves all swung toward the newcomer at the sound of his low voice. Not one of them, evidently, had sensed his approach.

"I sure can! My name is Andrew," he blurted out, relief pervading his being. He intuitively felt that the man in blue was someone he could rely upon. "I'm on my last legs. These wolves have been after me all day."

Yama strode toward the helpless traveler, seemingly unconcerned about the presence of the pack. "You look exhausted. I'll take you back to the Home with me."

"The Home!" Andrew exclaimed, and then stiffened in alarm when two of the wolves snarled and bounded at the intruder. "Look out!" he cried.

The warning proved unnecessary.

Displaying dazzling speed and consummate skill, the man called Yama assumed a squatting posture even as the scimitar flashed from its scabbard. The gleaming blade swung once, twice, both strokes nearly invisible to the naked eye, and with each swing a wolf toppled to the grass, blood spurting from its neck, almost decapitated. Yama straightened, his scimitar held vertical, the dripping blade next to his right cheek, and looked at the remaining wolves.

For a few seconds the pack returned the stare, then, one by one, they spun and raced for the woods to the southeast. They disappeared into the forest without so much as a backward glance.

"I don't believe it!" Andrew declared.

Yama squatted and wiped his scimitar on a dead wolf. "Wolves are intelligent creatures. They don't press a fight if they know they can't win.''

"Are you really from the Home?" Andrew asked.

"I'm not in the habit of lying," Yama said. He rose and replaced the scimitar in its scabbard.

"How did you know I was here?"

Yama shifted and pointed to the northwest. "The Warrior on the south wall saw you through his binoculars. I was target-shooting at the firing range, so he called down to me. I notified Blade, and he sent me to investigate."

Andrew gazed in the direction indicated and spied the top of a brick wall off in the distance. "Is that the Home?" he inquired eagerly.

"Yes."

"Then I've made it!" Andrew said in disbelief.

"You've been searching for the Home?" Yama questioned, and started to turn to lead the way.

"You don't know how hard and long I've been looking," Andrew replied. "I need—" he began, then froze in surprise when he saw the ebony silhouette of a skull stitched onto the fabric of Yama's uniform over the shoulder blades. "Why in the world do you have that skull on your back?"

"It's symbolic of my vocation."

"Huh?"

"I'll explain later," Yama said. "Right now we should get you to the Home. Your right side is bleeding."

Andrew glanced down. He had forgotten all about his wound in his excitement over being rescued from the pack. The wolf had torn his T-shirt and the flesh underneath, leaving a cut two inches long. "So it is," he responded. He walked over to the man in blue. "You saved my life. I'm in your debt."

"Any Warrior would have done the same."

"Are you a Warrior?"

"Yes."

An uncontrollable outburst of laughter erupted from Andrew and he slapped his left thigh in merriment.

"Did I say something funny?"

"No," Andrew replied, chuckling heartily. "Not at all."

"Then why are you laughing?" Yama asked.

"Because I've definitely come to the right place!"

Chapter One

The Home turned out to be a 30-acre compound enclosed within 20-foot-high brick walls topped by barbed wire. A drawbridge situated in the middle of the west wall afforded access to the stronghold. As Andrew crossed the bridge, spanning an inner moat, he gazed at the western section of the retreat in wonder. Six enormous concrete buildings were arranged in a triangular configuration and positioned one hundred yards apart. Dozens of people were in evidence. Men and women were talking or walking, many couples romantically linked arm in arm, while near the southernmost concrete building a group of musicians played a moving melody. Children played and laughed. "I've died and gone to Heaven," he declared in amazement.

Yama glanced quizzically at the thin man. "I beg your pardon?"

"This is incredible," Andrew said, and nodded at the tranquil scene. "Everyone looks so happy."

"Why shouldn't they be?"

Andrew snorted and jerked his left thumb at the drawbridge opening. "Do you know what life is like out there?"

"I've been into the Outlands."

"Then you must know how different your Home is from the

rest of the country. I mean, mutations and scavengers are everywhere. Even when a person lives in a relatively settled area near a big city, like I did on my farm near Green Bay, there's always the ever-present danger of being jumped while going about the daily chores,'' Andrew said, and sighed. ''All that damn radiation and chemical crap unleashed during the war really screwed up the world, didn't it?''

''No,'' Yama answered, heading toward the building positioned at the northwest corner of the triangle.

''No?'' Andrew repeated skeptically.

''Blame those who used the instruments of death, not the instruments themselves.''

Andrew pondered for a moment. ''Never thought of it quite that way before.''

''One of our Elders teaches a course on various aspects of World War Three, including an in-depth study of the causes and the military strategy of both sides,'' Yama mentioned. ''It's quite interesting.''

''Wait a minute. You're a Warrior, right? Isn't it your job to bust heads? And yet you attend classes? Do you mean you go to *school*?''

''My job, Andrew, is to defend the Home and protect the Family at all costs,'' Yama said, correcting him. ''And yes, I attend classes whenever I can. Everyone in the Family does. There's an ancient saying many of us have taken to heart: Use it or lose it. If we don't use our minds to better ourselves, we run the risk of becoming mental vegatables.'' He paused. ''Every child in the Family is required to attend formal schooling until he or she turns sixteen. After that, the classes are optional.''

''My folks taught me practically everything I know,'' Andrew said. ''Public schooling in America died with the war.''

''I know.''

Andrew looked at the building they were approaching. ''What is this place?''

''The infirmary,'' Yama divulged. ''Each of our Blocks, as

we call them, is devoted to a specific purpose. This is C Block. One of our Healers will tend to you.''

"I must speak with someone in authority. It's critically urgent," Andrew stated.

"Blade went to get Plato, the Family Leader. I'm sure they'll join us soon.''

"Who is this Blade you've mentioned?"

"The head Warrior.''

"From what I saw of you in action, I'm a bit surprised you're not the top Warrior," Andrew said.

Yama smiled. "Thanks for the compliment, but that honor is reserved for the very best Warrior in the entire Family.''

"And Blade is better than you?''

"Without a doubt.''

"I'll believe it when I see it," Andrew commented, and stared at the doorway to the infirmary. "Who built these buildings? They're gigantic.''

"The man we refer to as our Founder had the Home constructed according to his specifications. Kurt Carpenter was his name, and he was born about four decades before the outbreak of World War Three. He wisely foresaw that war would be inevitable, and he invested millions from his personal fortune to have the Home built. In Carpenter's time, forward-looking people like him were considered to be weird and labeled survivalists.''

Andrew nodded. "I know about survivalists," he said, pleased that the information he had received was proven to be accurate. He glanced at the many Family members milling about in the spacious area between the concrete Blocks, and noticed he had become the focus of attention. "A lot of them are staring at me.''

"You'll probably be the main topic of conversation over supper for most of the Family this evening.''

"How do they feel about outsiders?''

"It depends on the outsider. Scavengers and raiders are handled by the Warriors. Occasional visitors such as yourself must first demonstrate their trustworthiness before they're given the run of the compound," Yama said.

"But I walked into the Home without any problem," Andrew noted. "That guy with the strange haircut on the west wall never challenged me when I came over the moat. No one has interfered in any way. And you let me waltz in here carrying a rifle, for crying out loud."

"First of all, that guy on the west wall is Ares, a fellow Warrior. Don't allow his Mohawk haircut to fool you. He can riddle a tin can at one hundred yards. If you were believed to be an enemy, you would never have made it to the drawbridge. Second, it would be rude of the Family to badger you when you're obviously in need of medical attention and rest. Third, I don't see any reason why you can't bring an empty Winchester into the Home," Yama responded.

Andrew looked at the man in blue. "How did you know my rifle is empty?"

"Why else were you using it as a club instead of shooting at those wolves?" Yama rejoined. His voice lowered. "Besides, even if the Winchester was fully loaded, you're with me."

Andrew pursed his lips, appreciating the significance of the statement. After the incident with the wolves, he knew Yama could terminate him as readily as he might swat a fly. And if the other Warriors were equally as competent as the man beside him, then his plan just might succeed.

They came to the entrance to the infirmary and Yama paused to open the door. "I believe Nightingale is on duty," he commented, and stepped inside.

"Nightingale?" Andrew said. "Ares. Yama. No offense, but you people have unusual names." He stopped and studied the interior. Dozens of cots were aligned in two rows down the center of the chamber. Medical cabinets lined the walls. The sole occupant was a brown-haired woman dressed in white who sat at a desk near the doorway. She looked up and smiled.

"Hello, Yama. What have we here?"

"His name is Andrew," the Warrior replied. "Wolves tried to turn him into a snack."

The woman stood and motioned at the cot closest to the desk. "Have a seat, Andrew. I'll be right with you," she instructed him, then walked to a medicine cabinet along the west wall.

"So you think our names are unusual," Yama said.

"I've never heard them before," Andrew responded as he moved to the cot and slowly, wearily, sat down.

"You must not do much reading."

"I can read," Andrew stated. "But I never have the time. And too, we only own a few books. They're hard to come by, you know."

"The Family possesses hundreds of thousands of books in our library in E Block."

"Really? Hundreds of thousands?"

"And every volume was stocked by Kurt Carpenter. There are history books. Geography books. How-to books. Fiction. Nonfiction. You name it, it's probably in our library," Yama elaborated. "Most of us have taken our names from those books."

"What?"

"Our Founder instituted a formal Naming ceremony for every Family member when he or she turns sixteen. Carpenter was afraid his followers and descendants would lose sight of the factors contributing to the holocaust, so he started the Naming as a way of encouraging them to stay in touch with their roots. Originally, names were only taken from historical volumes. Later, the practice was expanded to include any type of book. Some Family members have even adopted a new name of their own choosing, like Blade."

"Where did you take your name from?" Andrew inquired.

"The Hindu King of Death."

"Why would—" Andrew began to say, then thought better of the question, recalling vividly the two slain wolves.

"Here we are," Nightingale announced, returning with a first-aid kit and a large bottle of antiseptic. She knelt in front of the cot and inspected the wound. "You have quite a nasty bite there."

"Don't I know it."

"I'll clean the cut and stitch it for you," Nightingale offered. "You'll be as good as new in no time."

"I don't want to put you to any bother."

"Nonsense. I'm a Healer. Ministering to the sick and the injured is my job."

Andrew gazed at the rows of empty cots. "You don't have very many patients."

Nightingale placed the first-aid kit on the cot and opened the lid. "Not at the moment, no. By and large, the Family is blessed with abundant health."

"But how can all of you be so healthy? Disease is widespread in the Outlands."

"So I've been told," Nightingale said. She removed a box of cotton balls and set it alongside the kit. "Fortunately, our Tillers and Hunters provide us with the vegetables, grains, and meat we need to have a nutritional diet. We don't have the proper climate to grow abundant fruit, but the Tillers do their best during the growing season and supply us with apples, pears, and others." She pause to unscrew the cap on the antiseptic. "With the proper diet and regular exercise, maintaining optimum health is a simple task."

"If you say so," Andrew replied, "but I'm a farmer, lady. I grow crops for a living and so do my friends. We eat better than most in the Outlands, but we still come down with disease from time to time."

"Are you afflicted with negative attitudes?"

"What do our attitudes have to do with anything?"

"Plenty. Our Elders teach that our attitude can literally make the difference between life and death."

"It sounds as if these Elders of yours spend all their time spouting words of wisdom," Andrew quipped.

"Doesn't it make sense to benefit from the seasoned experience of those who are older than you are?" Nightingale asked.

"Yeah. I guess you have a point. But I get the impression the Family has put their Elders on pedestals."

"We respect their judgment. We don't worship them," Nightingale said. "Now would you be so kind as to take off your shirt?"

"No problem," Andrew assured her. He placed the Winchester on the cot to his right, then gingerly stripped off his torn T-shirt, wincing as sharp pangs stabbed his right side. "Is everyone at the Home the same as you two?"

"How do you mean?" the Healer queried, examining the bite carefully.

"I don't know how to describe it, but you're different than most folks I know. Are you sure you're from this planet?"

Nightingale smiled. "We *don't* have negative attitudes." She applied antiseptic to a cotton ball and dabbed at the wound. "This might sting a little," she warned.

Andrew grunted and flinched. "Just a tad." He watched her clean the cut, then did a double-take when she removed a thin needle from the first-aid kit. "What's that for?"

"What do you think it's for?" Nightingale rejoined. She took a roll of shiny thread from the kit. "This is nonabsorbable silk material which is used in making sutures. I'm going to sew the torn skin back together."

"Couldn't we just let it heal naturally?"

"You're not afraid, are you?"

"Who, me?" Andrew responded nervously, and addressed Yama to distract himself from the mental image of the needle penetrating his flesh. "So tell me. How many Warriors are there?"

"There are currently seventeen," Yama said, and frowned. "We lost one two months ago and a replacement hasn't been selected yet."

"I'm sorry to hear that," Andrew said out of courtesy. "So there are normally eighteen, all told?"

"There have been ever since the three hybrids were permitted to join the Warrior ranks."

"Hybrids? Do you mean mutations?"

"Yes."

Andrew's surprise showed. "You have mutant Warriors?"

"Lynx, Ferret, and Gremlin were genetically engineered by

the infamous Doktor. They rebelled against him and joined us in our war against the madman. They're outstanding Warriors."

"I'll bet the damn Doktor isn't the only one your Family has had trouble with," Andrew commented, hoping to sound the Warrior out, to prompt Yama to relate the details of the conflict with the Technics.

"There have been others," Yama admitted.

Andrew waited for additional details, but when the man in blue simply stood there observing the Healer, he decided to take the initiative. "I was told that the Family had a run-in with the Technics once," he said, and was startled to see the big man's features harden.

"Yes," Yama laconically replied, the word almost a hiss.

Andrew opened his mouth, about to question Yama further, when two events occurred simultaneously that completely derailed his train of thought. The Healer, without warning, began to insert the needle into his skin just as a veritable giant strolled into the infirmary.

Chapter Two

"Son of a bitch!" Andrew blurted out, and recoiled from the needle, his wide eyes locked on the new arrival.

The giant stood seven feet in height and possessed a truly herculean build. He wore a black leather vest, green fatigue pants, and combat boots, and his exposed arms, shoulders, and abdomen rippled with layers of bulging muscles. He radiated an almost palpable aura of power and virility. A comma of dark hair hung above his gray eyes. Strapped around his lean waist were a matched pair of Bowie knives. He came directly over to the cot.

Yama had swiveled to face the giant. "Here he is, Blade."

Blade halted and placed his brawny hands on his Bowies. "What's your name?" he asked in a husky voice.

"Andrew, sir."

"Your whole name?"

"Andrew Wolski, sir," Andrew said, awed by the head Warrior's intimidating presence. He'd seen some large men in his time, and had deemed Yama to be one of the largest, but this titan made all the others seem like midgets, and even surpassed the man in blue.

"Call me Blade," the giant said.

"Yes, sir."

"And stop calling me sir."

"Whatever you say. Anything you want, you get."

"How accommodating of you, Andrew," stated a gray-haired man who stepped from behind Blade, smiling pleasantly. "I'm Plato, the Family Leader."

"Pleased to meet you," Andrew said, noting the kindly, weathered visage on the man who might well determine the fate of his wife and daughter. The Leader wore a green shirt and faded corduroy pants, and sported a full gray beard to complement his shoulder-length hair. "I must talk to you right away."

"Certainly," Plato said.

"I'd like to stitch this wolf bite first," Nightingale interjected.

"In a minute," Blade told her, studying the thin man from head to toe. "Is he packing?" he asked.

"Just the rifle," Yama answered.

Blade nodded, his gray eyes boring into Wolski. "Who sent you?"

"What?"

"Who sent you here?"

Andrew blinked a few times, disturbed by the edge of the giant's tone. "Nobody. I came here on my own. I've been looking for the Home for weeks."

"Where are you from?"

"I live on a small farm west of Green Bay, Wisconsin."

"Then you claim you're a farmer?"

Andrew straightened, his eyes narrowing. "I *am* a farmer," he asserted indignantly. "What else would I be?"

"An assassin," Blade said.

"A what?" Andrew declared in disbelief.

"An assassin. The Family has made a number of enemies, any one of whom would go to great lengths to kill Plato and myself," Blade stated. "You might be an assassin sent here to eliminate us."

"But I'm not," Andrew protested vigorously.

"Prove it," Blade told him, his right hand sweeping up and

out, drawing his right Bowie. He lanced the knife at the thin man's neck.

Fear flooded through Andrew. He saw the glistening tip coming at his throat and he frantically tried to throw himself to the left. Dizziness assailed him as all the blood seemed to abruptly drain from his face. His frayed emotional state, his weariness and hunger all conspired to produce an unexpected effect. He fainted, sinking onto his side on the cot.

Several seconds of silence elapsed.

"I guess he isn't a professional assassin," Yama remarked and laughed.

"That was cruel," Nightingale said. "You scared the poor man half to death."

"I agree," Plato concurred. He glanced at Blade. "Was such a barbaric act necessary?"

"We needed to be sure," the head Warrior responded. "I can't take any chances where your life is concerned." He slowly sheathed the Bowie and looked at Nightingale. "Stitch him up while he's unconscious. I want to be informed the minute he wakes up."

"Will do," she promised.

Plato turned to Yama. "Did he give you any clue as to his reason for seeking us out?"

"He wanted to talk to someone in authority," Yama related, and his countenance clouded. "He mentioned the Technics."

"He did, did he?" Blade remarked thoughtfully. "I'll post a guard to stay here until he revives."

"I'd like to volunteer," Yama offered.

"Isn't this your day off?"

"I don't mind."

Blade absently stroked his chin. "I thought you were busy with target practice."

"The firing range can wait. I want to keep an eye on our visitor," Yama said.

"Suit yourself. Bring him outside after Nightingale is finished," Blade ordered. He turned and walked to the doorway,

Plato trailing behind him. They sauntered toward the moat.

"Yama has developed an inordinate interest in Andrew Wolski," Plato remarked when they were ten yards from C Block. "He must suspect that the Technics are somehow involved with Mister Wolski."

"Or Yama *hopes* they are," Blade amended. "If I read Wolski correctly, he's here to ask our help. Yama must believe the same thing, and I gather he's hoping the Technics are the culprits. He wants a chance to get his revenge."

"I've always considered Yama to be one of the finest Warriors. He exhibits superb self-control. I should think he had gotten over her by now," Plato said.

"How do you get over the death of a loved one?"

The Family Leader clasped his bony hands behind his back and sighed. "I see your point. What will you do?"

"I'll cross that bridge when I come to it," Blade said. He gazed at the azure sky, then at the rampart on the west wall where Ares stood with a Colt AR-15 slung over his left shoulder. "We have something else to discuss."

"The replacement for Marcus?"

"Exactly. I've selected a candidate to formally sponsor before the Elders."

Plato glanced at his companion fondly, remembering the day, years ago, when Blade's father had been slain by a mutate and Plato had decided to take the youth under his wing. He viewed the giant as the son he'd never had, and he had appointed Blade as the chief Warrior after assuming the post of Leader. "I was wondering when you were going to get around to nominating someone. Several of the other Elders have commented on the delay."

"I've delayed choosing a candidate because I wanted to carefully evaluate those who are qualified for the post. After what happened to Marcus, I want to make the right choice."

"Marcus died because he was inexperienced. No matter who you pick now, they'll be equally as inexperienced," Plato said.

"True. But I'm hoping to select a candidate who will be more decisive than Marcus, someone who can think fast under stress,'' Blade stated, and paused. "I know several of the Warriors have sponsored their own favorite candidates.''

"Yes, Rikki-Tikki-Tavi is sponsoring Norris. Spartacus has nominated Jason. And Sundance is sponsoring Mather.''

"You're kidding.''

Plato chuckled. "I wish I was. None of the Elders view Mather as a serious candidate. He's too unstable. But what about you? The person you sponsor will be the heavy favorite. Your recommendation carries a lot of weight with the Elders.''

"I know.' Which is another reason I wanted the ideal nominee.''

"So how long do you intend to keep me in suspense?''

Blade looked at his mentor and grinned. "I plan to sponsor Achilles.''

The Family Leader suddenly halted, then checked to ensure none of the other Family members were within hearing range. "Now you're the one who is kidding, I trust.''

"Nope,'' Blade replied, resting his hands on his hips.

"Achilles?'' Plato repeated the name, speaking with the same inflection he might employ to discuss a plague.

"What's wrong with him? His Tegner instructor reports that Achilles has mastered karate,'' Blade said, referring to the Elder responsible for teaching the martial arts. Among the countless books in the Family library were two dozen on hand-to-hand combat written by a man named Bruce Tegner. Each of the books contained precise, detailed instructions and diagrams, and included photographs of each stance, position, and movement. There were Tegner books on karate, judo, jujitsu, aikido, kung fu, savate, jukado, and many other styles of martial combat. The Tegner books were used as the basic source of tutelage in unarmed fighting, and the training classes, which were taught by an Elder who was a former Warrior, had become known as Tegner sessions, or simply Tegner.

Plato nodded. "I've heard that Achilles is almost as skilled as Rikki and Yama.''

"And Achilles has qualified as a marksman,'' Blade noted. "He's a whiz with an Uzi.''

"True," Plato conceded.

"Achilles is quick and he's deadly. I believe he'll make an outstanding Warrior."

"But what about his compatibility with the other Warriors?" Plato inquired. "Achilles has a certain knack for rubbing people the wrong way, as you well know. He's opinionated, pompous, and egotistical."

Blade shrugged. "Everyone has character flaws."

"But Warriors should have as few as possible," Plato stated. "Why do you think the Founder implemented such a rigorous screening process for Warrior candidates? The Elders have long prided themselves on choosing only superior nominees. Oh, a few mistakes have been made in the last century. Napoleon was a case in point. Overall, though, our record is exemplary." He shook his head. "I'm amazed that you would contemplate sponsoring Achilles."

"I'm not *contemplating* sponsoring him," Blade said. "I've already made up my mind to submit his name."

Plato's forehead furrowed and he scrutinized the giant's face, reading determination in the set of Blade's features. "If you've already decided, then nothing I can say will dissuade you. But be advised. The Elders might reject Achilles. His nomination will spark a bitter debate."

"I just hope the Elders will judge Achilles objectively and not allow their personal feelings to interfere with their better judgment."

"We'll do our best," Plato said dryly.

"Good. Now that that's settled, there's another subject I need to bring up," Blade mentioned.

"Should I brace myself?"

Blade smiled. "I want to discuss perimeter security."

"What is there to discuss? We always have three Warriors patrolling the ramparts, and we keep the land cleared of all boulders, brush, and trees for one hundred and fifty yards in every direction from the four walls. Our perimeter security is adequate."

"Is it? The Trolls managed to invade the Home once, if you'll recall. A Technic demolition squad reached the top of the west wall before they were stopped. And the pair of hybrid assassins sent by the Doktor sneaked in and killed a Tiller,'' Blade said.

''The Trolls were successful because we had grown complacent after so many years without an attack. Those hybrids came through the aqueduct at the northwest corner of the Home. Since then, we've installed heavy screens over the aqueduct to prevent anyone or anything from swimming in,'' Plato responded, and gazed at the water flowing along the base of the west wall. ''The Founder diverted the stream into the Home and channeled it all along the inside of the walls as a secondary line of defense. He didn't foresee that enemies might use the aqueducts to infiltrate the Home.''

Blade watched a group of children who were playing tag in the commons area between the Blocks. ''The important point isn't how our security was breached, but the fact that a breach occurred. I propose to upgrade our defenses with a Canine Team.''

''A what?''

''I've seen them in California. A handler and a dog, usually a German shepherd or a Doberman pinscher, work in tandem. The dogs go through extensive training and they're outstanding guards.''

Plato listened attentively. The Free State of California was an ally of the Family's. They were but two of seven organized factions comprising the Freedom Federation, an alliance of scattered pockets of civilization in a world driven insane by the nuclear Armageddon. In addition to California, the Family had signed a mutual self-defense treaty with the Flathead Indians, who now controlled the state of Montana; with the Cavalry, a rugged population of superb horsemen and frontiersmen who governed the Dakota Territory; with the Moles, a reclusive group who dwelt in an undergrond city in north-central Minnesota; with the Clan, refugees from the ravaged Twin Cities who had relocated in Halma, near the Home; and with the Civilized Zone. Of all the factions, only the Civilized Zone could rightfully lay claim to being the direct administrative successor of the United States of America. During the war the U.S. government had evacuated thousands and thousands of its citizens into the area formerly embracing the states of Kansas, Nebraska, Colorado, Wyoming, New Mexico, and Oklahoma and portions of Arizona and the northern half of Texas. After the government had collapsed, a dictatorship had arisen and the dictator had renamed the Midwest region and selected Denver, Colorado, to be the new capital.

"Governor Melnick has offered to send us a half-dozen dogs," Blade was saying, "as a token of appreciation for the friendship between California and the Family. I'm thinking of accepting. The Dobermans and German shepherds would be a definite asset."

"But who would handle the canines?" Plato asked. "The Warriors already have ample responsibilities."

"I had this brainstorm," Blade said. "What if we took six inexperienced candidates, six younger members of the Family who want to become Warriors, and paired them with dogs. We could train them to work with the Dobermans and shepherds and assign them to patrolling the perimeter. This way, we wouldn't jeopardize our security by depleting our regular Warrior ranks, and we would be giving potential Warriors the opportunity to gain needed experience."

Plato nodded slowly, once again impressed by the clarity of logic his apprentice demonstrated. "Your idea has merit. Would the novice Warriors be accorded full Warrior status?"

"No. We'll think up an appropriate title."

"And what about Achilles? Will he be assigned to the Canine Team?" Plato questioned.

Blade shook his head. "I want him to be accepted as a full-fledged Warrior."

"I don't see why you are so insistent."

"Trust me," Blade said.

Plato looked the giant in the eyes. "You know I do." He coughed lightly. "So when will you submit your proposal to the Elders?"

"At the next meeting. If the Elders agree, I'll relay the word to Governor Melnick on my next trip to Los Angeles.''

"Which will be when?''

Blade turned and stared at C Block. "I don't know. I intended to head back in a few days, but my trip may be delayed by our friend in there.''

"What if he journeyed so far to request our assistance? Will you relay his plea to the Federation Council? This might turn out to be a job for the Force, not the Warriors.''

"Maybe," Blade conceded. The Federation leaders had formed an elite tactical unit composed of a volunteer from each Federation faction and dubbed this unit the Freedom Force. Whenever the leaders received word of a possible threat to the safety of the Federation, the Force was dispatched to investigate and deal with the problem, if necessary. Due to his widely acknowledged expertise in such matters, Blade had been picked to be the head of the Force. He now spent, on average, a week out of each month in Los Angeles, where the Force facility was located, and the remaining three weeks at the Home with his wife and son. If an emergency arose during those weeks, the governor of California would immediately dispatch a Hurricane, a jet possessing vertical-takeoff-and-landing capibility, to pick him up. The VTOLs normally flew a regular shuttle service between the Federation factions. "We won't know until we talk to him.''

"I hope, for your sake, that the reason for his being here won't entail another run into the Outlands.''

Blade made a snorting noise. "Ever heard of a guy named Murphy?''

Chapter Three

"How are you feeling?" Plato inquired.

"Much better, thank you," Andrew Wolski replied. He lay on the cot with three plump white pillows propped under his shoulders. "That Healer did a great job of bandaging me up. And after the venison soup I ate, I feel terrific."

"Then you're ready to talk?"

"I was ready when I got here, but I wasn't in the best of shape," Andrew said. To his left stood the Family Leader. On his right, side by side, were the giant and the man in blue.

"You mentioned that you came looking for us," Blade stated. "Why?"

Andrew frowned and closed his eyes for a moment. When he opened them and gazed at the head Warrior, they were filled with a profound inner sadness. "It's my wife and daughter. I need your help or they'll die."

Blade and Plato exchanged glances.

"Start at the beginning," the giant directed. "Tell us everything."

"Okay. You'll need some background first," Andrew said, and launched into his tale. "I've been a farmer all of my life. I was raised on a farm west of Green Bay, and I took over the farm after my parents were killed in a freak accident. They were coming back from a neighbor's in a buggy and something must have spooked their team. When they didn't return on time, a search got underway.'' He paused. ''We found the buggy smashed to bits against a tree. Their bodies were in the wreckage.''

''Do you have any brothers or sisters?'' Plato tactfully asked, hoping to take Wolski's mind off the tragic mishap.

''One of each,'' Andrew responded. ''My sister married a guy who lives about twenty miles from our place. He's a farmer too. My younger brother tired of the farming life and took off. I don't know if he ever found what he was looking for because I never heard from him again.''

''How long ago did he leave?'' Plato queried.

''Sixteen years ago. I expect he's dead by now.''

''How does all of this relate to your wife and daughter?'' Blade interjected.

Andrew looked up. ''I'm getting to that. Fourteen years ago I met the most beautiful woman who ever lived, Sandra. And I don't mean the kind of beauty that's only skin deep either. She's beautiful inside, where it really counts.''

''Any man who finds the ideal love of his life is indeed fortunate,'' Plato commented.

''Sandra and I were inseparable. I live just to make her happy,'' Andrew said. ''Our daughter, Nadine, was born nine months after our wedding. She's our only child. Not that we haven't tried to have more.''

''And Sandra and Nadine are in danger?'' Blade prompted.

Andrew nodded. ''The Mad Scientist has them.''

The giant's eyebrows arched. ''The who?''

''The Mad Scientist is the name we've given to the bastard who showed up in Green Bay about six months ago,'' Andrew disclosed. ''You see, until the madman arrived, we didn't have any major problems. Oh, we had our share of scavengers and mutations and whatnot. But not the sheer terror we have now. We grew our crops and traded for whatever we needed with the Indians and the townspeople.''

''Just a second,'' Plato interrupted. ''There are a few facts that require clarification. Who controls Green Bay?''

"The Mad Scientist does now, but before he came no one did. There were people living there, but they weren't very organized. They lived hand to mouth by scrounging items they found in all the abandoned buildings. Green Bay wasn't hit during the war, but most of the folks left. My grandfather told me they were forced to leave by the government and taken somewhere else. The city is rundown. Most of the stores and houses are falling apart. Rats and cockroaches are everywhere,'' Andrew said distastefully. "I don't see how anyone could live there.''

"Where do the Indians live?'' Plato probed.

"I wish I had a map,'' Andrew stated.

"We can get one,'' Blade offered.

"I won't need it. Just follow me on this. The city of Green Bay is located at the south end of Green Bay. Due west of the city—bordering it, in fact—is the Oneida Indian Reservation, which is only about ten miles wide. Just west of the Reservation, near a deserted town called Seymour, is where I have my farm.''

"I take it the Oneida Indians stayed on the reservations after the war?'' Plato inquired.

"Most did. They don't like to refer to it as a reservation, though. To them, it's just their land. They're very peaceful and have never caused any trouble for the farmers and ranchers.''

"Go on with your story,'' Plato said.

"Okay. About six months ago a rumor started circulating that a strange man had shown up in Green Bay with an escort of forty soldiers and taken over the old University of Wisconsin campus.''

"Soldiers?'' Blade repeated.

"Yeah.'' Andrew nodded. "Technics.''

For the first time since the conversation commenced, Yama stirred. He straightened and stepped closer to the cot. "How do you know these soldiers are Technics?''

"The farmers in my area deal with the Technics on a regular basis. Those sons of bitches are always in the market for food to feed the people they have crammed in Technic City. We know Technic soldiers when we see them,'' Andrew assured him. ''Anyway, the guy who took over the college had a barbed-wire fence erected and signs posted to keep everyone out. He warned the people living in the city to stay away under penalty of death.''

''What is this guy's name?'' Blade queried.

''No one knows. He's real secretive. All we do know is that he's involved in some kind of scientific research. That's why everybody started calling him the Mad Scientist.''

''How do you know he's engaged in research?'' Plato questioned.

''Because he let it slip. When he first arrived, some of the city folk went to pay him a visit. He joked that if they didn't mind their own business, they'd be sorry. Told them the research he was doing might be contagious, then laughed.''

''You're certain about this?'' Plato asked, pressing him.

''Positive. I talked to a couple who were there.''

Yama leaned forward. ''And you're sure this scientist is tied in with the Technics?''

Andrew scowled. ''How many times do I have to tell you? Let me spell it out. Green Bay drains into Lake Michigan, in case you didn't know, and on the south end of Lake Michigan, only two hundred miles away, is Technic city. Or Chicago, as they used to call it. The Technics have contacted farmers all along the lake, offering to trade for crops. I've dealt with them dozens of times.''

Oddly, Yama smiled and seemed to relax. ''Excellent,'' he remarked cryptically.

''What puzzles me is why the Technics would establish a research station in Green Bay,'' Plato said. ''What does the University of Wisconsin have to offer that the Technics don't already have in Technic City? They adulate technology and science. Their own research facilities must be some of the best on the planet.''

''I wish I could answer that,'' Andrew said. ''But no one has a clue as to what those slime are up to.''

"If you think they're slime, why did you deal with them?" Blade asked.

Andrew shrugged. "I couldn't afford to be choosy. The Technics could supply clothes, tools, kerosene, matches, and a whole lot of other stuff that was hard to come by otherwise."

"You still haven't told us how your wife and daughter are in danger," Blade noted.

The farmer's shoulders sagged. "They've disappeared."

"Explain," Blade said.

"About a month after the Technic scientist arrived, people began to vanish. At first, no one wanted to believe the reports. When some of the folks living in the city disappeared, and the stories started circulating, everyone assumed the missing persons had left because they didn't want to be anywhere near the creepy scientist. Then more and more people vanished into thin air. City folks. Indians. And even some of my neighbors."

"Didn't anyone do anything?" Blade asked.

"What could we do? We had three choices. We could march up to the barbed-wire fence and demand to know what was going on, in which case the Technics would have shot us. We could pack our belongings and get the hell out of there. Or we could stay and hope for the best," Andrew said. "Most of my neighbors were in the same boat I was in. We had too much invested in our property to run off."

"How many persons have disappeared, all told?" Blade inquired.

"As near as I could guess, and bear in mind this was three weeks ago, over thirty people have vanished without a trace."

"What happened to your wife and daughter?"

Andrew slumped into the pillows, his sorrow self-evident. "Three weeks ago, about an hour before sunset, a neighbor's son rode over to our place and let me know that his dad had busted a leg. My neighbor, Ed, had fallen off a ladder while cleaning a gutter on his house. He needed someone to help set the broken bones, so I rode over with the son." He stopped and took a deep breath. "Two hours later, when I got home, no one was there. Sandra and Nadine weren't anywhere to be found. Everything in our house was in perfect order. None of the furniture was disturbed, and there was no sign of a struggle. Supper was simmering on the stove. I scoured our house from the attic to the basement, but my wife and daughter had disappeared.''

Blade crossed his arms on his chest, the corners of his mouth curling downward. He could sympathize with the farmer. If anything ever happened to his beloved Jenny and little Gabe, he'd be devastated.

''I went crazy,'' Andrew went on. ''I called my neighbors together and we searched every square inch of my farm. No one found a clue. But I knew it had to have been the Technics who were responsible. I wanted to go to the University and demand to see the man in charge, but my friends talked me out of the idea. They told me that I'd be committing suicide, that it wouldn't help Sandra and Nadine one bit.'' He fell silent, his eyes moistening.

''Take your time,'' Plato said. ''We can wait.''

Andrew cleared his throat. ''There's not too much left to tell. I was frantic. I tried to organize my friends and the Indians to go after my wife and daughter, but they wouldn't agree. They were scared. I can't say as I blame them.''

''When did you decide to come here?'' Blade queried.

''Four days after Sandra and Nadine vanished, I saddled up my mare, packed all the supplies I figured I'd need, and lit out. All went well until seven days ago. A band of scavengers ambushed me. My mare was killed and I barely got away with my life. I decided to keep going, no matter what. And here I am,'' Andrew concluded.

''Back up a bit,'' Blade said. ''Why did you decide to come to the Home? Why *us*?''

''Because I'd heard stories about how the Family had tangled with with the damn Technics and won. A Warrior reportedly killed the Technic Minister and his First Secretary. Technic City was in turmoil for weeks. I first heard about it from a drunk at a tavern.''

''Where did he hear the story?''

"From some Technic soldiers who had stopped there to wet their whistles," Andrew replied. "Naturally, when my wife and daughter were taken, when I desperately needed aid, I thought of the Family. You're the only ones I know of who have ever beaten the Technics. Everyone else is too afraid to take the bastards on."

"What do you want us to do?" Blade asked.

"Let your Warriors come to Green Bay with me. Help me find Sandra and Nadine."

Blade lowered his arms. "Your wife and daughter have been missing for three weeks. As difficult as it might be to accept, they could be dead by now."

"They could still be alive," Andrew said, his voice strained. "I believe they are. Call it wishful thinking if you want, but deep down inside I know Sandra and Nadine haven't been killed. Yet."

"You ask a lot of us," Blade stated softly.

"I don't have anyone else I can turn to," Andrew responded plaintively. "You're my last hope."

"I say we go," Yama unexpectedly declared.

Blade glanced at his fellow Warrior. "The decision is mine to make, not yours."

"I know," Yama said. "I mean no disrespect. And if you decide not to assist him, then I'd like to request a leave of absence so I can return to Green Bay with him."

"You'd do that for me?" Andrew blurted.

Yama looked at the farmer. "For both of us."

"I don't understand," Andrew said, puzzled by the intensity of Yama's expression.

"First things first," Plato interjected authoritatively. "Blade and I must discuss your appeal."

"Whatever you want," the farmer stated.

Plato headed for the doorway. "Blade, would you join me outside?"

"In a minute," Blade responded. He faced Yama. "I know what you went through, but I'm not about to let you go traipsing off by yourself. A Warrior should never allow his actions to

be dominated by his emotions. You know as well as I do that going into combat with your head clouded by hatred will make you careless. And carelessness can make you dead."

"I don't hate them."

"Oh? You could have fooled me. If it isn't hatred, then it's the next best thing."

Andrew shifted on the cot. "What is this all about?"

"None of your business," Yama snapped.

"Oh."

"See what I mean?" Blade queried. "You wouldn't last ten seconds."

"Have I ever failed to perform my duties properly?" Yama asked earnestly.

"No. But there's always a first time."

"At least give me the benefit of the doubt."

"I won't stand by and let you kill yourself."

"Fair enough. But if you decide to go, and I expect you will, I'd like to go along," Yama said. "You know how much this means to me. If the situation were reversed, if it had happened to you, you'd be the first one over the drawbridge."

Blade went to reply, then changed his mind. Yama had a valid point. "I'll think about it," he offered, and strode from the infirmary.

Plato stood 20 feet off, his countenance troubled, absently tugging at his beard. He looked up as the giant approached, and sighed. "You have to go. You know that, don't you?"

"I know," Blade stated stiffly.

"If the Technics are hatching a new plot, we must discover their plan. The future safety of the Family is at stake."

"I know."

The Family Leader gestured at C Block. "And although the very notion runs counter to my better judgment, I believe you owe it to Yama to take him along."

"I know," Blade said yet again, then added harshly, "Damn!"

"How many other Warriors will you take with you?"

"Just one."

"Are you certain three Warriors will be enough?"

"Every Warrior I take reduces our defensive capability that much more. Usually only three Warriors go on a run, and I see no need to change the procedure this time around," Blade said.

"Who will you take then? Hickok?"

"No. Hickok will be in charge of the Warriors while I'm gone. I have someone else in mind, someone who can help keep Yama in line," Blade answered.

Plato's brow knit, and he pondered for several seconds. He gazed to the west, in the direction of the dozens of log cabins aligned from north to south in the center of the compound, and nodded. "Oh. An appropriate choice."

"Who else?"

Chapter Four

"So what's the name of this vehicle again?" Andrew asked.

"The SEAL," Blade responded, his eyes on the stretch of State Highway 46 ahead, his hands gripping the steering wheel lightly. Cracks, ruts, potholes, and an occasional crater several feet deep had transformed the highway into an obstacle course. Although the SEAL could negotiate any type of terrain with relative ease, he skillfully avoided the craters to spare his passengers from being unduly jostled. The air coming through his open window stirred his hair.

"Why would anyone name a gigantic van after an animal that swims around in the water?" Andrew queried.

"SEAL is an acronym. It stands for Solar Energized Amphibious and Land Recreational Vehicle."

"Recreational?"

"Yeah. Kurt Carpenter spent millions of dollars to have the transport developed by automakers in Detroit before the war. Carpenter foresaw the collapse of mass transportation. He knew the Family would have need of a special type of vehicle. So he had the SEAL built according to his specifications. The automakers viewed him as a harmless eccentric with gobs of money," Blade elaborated, feeling grateful for his ancestor's wisdom. Without the SEAL to convey them long distances, the

Family would never have ventured into the outside world and met their allies in the Federation.

As a prototype, the SEAL incorporated revolutionary design elements in its construction. As its name denoted, the van was solar-powered. A pair of solar panels attached to the roof collected the sunlight, which was converted and stored in unique batteries housed in a lead-lined case under the SEAL. Fabricated to be virtually indestructible, the body of the vehicle consisted of a shatterproof, heat-resistant plastic, and the floor was composed of an impervious metal alloy. To traverse the roughest landscape, the van rode on four huge tires, each four feet high, two feet wide, and puncture-resistant.

"But what happens if we run into trouble?" Andrew inquired. "What good is a recreational vehicle against armed enemies?"

Blade smiled. "Any enemy who attacks the SEAL is in for a big surprise," he said, thinking of the special modifications the Founder had made on the transport. Or rather, Carpenter had hired mercenaries to make the modifications. Four toggle switches located on the dash would activate the SEAL's armaments. Hidden under each front headlight in a recessed compartment was a 50-caliber machine gun. Mounted in the roof over the driver's seat was a minaturized surface-to-air missile, a heat-seeking Stinger with a range of ten miles. An Army Surplus Model flamethrower had been installed in the middle of the front fender. Layers of insulation surrounded the flamethrower to protect the vehicle from the extreme heat when the device was triggered. And finally, a rocket launcher had been placed in the center of the front grill.

"I've never seen a vehicle like this one," Andrew said. He glanced to his left at the giant, who sat behind the wheel in the other bucket seat. A console separated them. "Why is the body tinted green?"

"So we can see out but no one can see inside," Blade answered. "Carpenter didn't miss a trick."

"The Lord blessed us with a provident Founder," commented a deep voice to his rear.

Blade looked into the rearview mirror. Behind the bucket seats was another seat running the width of the vehicle. Yama sat on the passenger side, morosely staring out at the countryside. Under the silver-haired Warrior's left arm rested a Smith and Wesson Model 586 Distinguished Combat Magnum; under his right arm a Browning Hi-Power 9-millimeter Automatic Pistol. Dangling from Yama's right hip was a Razorback survival knife, and from the left side his scimitar. Cradled in his lap was a Wilkinson Carbine fitted with a 50-shot magazine.

Directly behind Blade sat the speaker. He wore a camouflage uniform tailored to fit by the Family Weavers, and the snug fabric accentuated his massive, broad-shouldered build. His eyes were brown, his features ruggedly handsome. His square jaw lent him an aspect of forceful decisiveness. But his most striking feature was his light brown hair, which hung to the small of his wide back and had been braided from the neck down. A pair of Bushmaster Auto Pistols were strapped to his waist, each one in a specially crafted swivel holster. Propped against his right leg was a Bushmaster Auto Rifle. In size and stature he appeared to be Yama's twin, although at six feet three inches he stood a shade shorter than the man in blue. His musculature, however, had been developed to a slightly higher degree and he was thicker through the middle.

"This is the first extended run you've been on, Samson," Blade remarked. "How do you like it so far?"

Samson patted the seat. "It's a cushy job. We have all the comforts of home. No wonder Hickok and Geronimo like to take off with you all the time."

"Enjoy the peace and quiet while it lasts," Blade advised, and glanced at Yama. "What about you? How are you holding up?"

"I'm bored to tears. I can't wait to reach Green Bay."

Andrew twisted in his seat. "You wouldn't say that if you knew the Technics like I know the Technics."

Yama's lips became a thin line. "I know them."

"Were you involved with the run-in your Family had with them?" Andrew inquired.

Yama simply nodded.

"Say! Were you the one who killed the Minister and the First Secretary?"

"No," Yama responded.

"Hickok was the Warrior who took care of the Minister," Blade disclosed.

"Wasn't he the one I met right before we left? The guy wearing the buckskins? The one who talked funny?" Andrew queried.

Blade grinned. "That was Hickok."

"He's weird."

"So everyone keeps telling me."

Andrew looked at the silver-haired Warrior, puzzled by Yama's moody behavior, then turned his attention to the one they called Samson. "Do you mind if I ask you a question?"

"Be my guest, brother."

"Why do you wear your hair so long? Doesn't it get in your way when you're fighting?"

Samson chuckled and reached back to pull his braided locks over his left shoulder. "I wear my hair in this style because I'm a Nazarite."

"A Nazarite? I thought you were a Warrior," Andrew mentioned.

"I'm both."

"So what's a Nazarite? The name sounds vaguely familiar."

"Have you read the Bible?" Samson asked.

"Parts of it," Andrew said.

"Well, the order of the voluntary Nazarites stems from Biblical times. I took the Nazarite vow when I was seven, pledging to live according to the will of the Lord, every second of every day. As a token of that vow, as a symbol of my devotion, I've never let a razor touch the hair on my head," Samson detailed.

The farmer blinked a few times, glanced at Blade, then at Samson. "Are you putting me on?"

"I would never mock the Lord."

"Wow. I've never heard of anyone doing such a thing," Andrew stated.

"The original Samson, the one in the Bible who slew the Philistines, was a Nazarite. So was John the Baptist. I've merely carried on the tradition," Samson said.

"I believe in God, but you must *really* be religious to go this far. What else is part of your vow?"

"I've never drunk intoxicating beverages."

"Never?" Andrew asked, and idly brushed at a dirt smudge on the blue shirt the Family had given him, along with pants and a box of ammo.

"If I permit alcohol to touch my lips, I violate my vow," Samson explained. "And if I break my pledge, I will break the spiritual bond linking me to our Maker. If that were to happen I'd lost my strength and power."

Andrew did a double take. "You don't really believe that, do you?"

"With all my heart, mind, and soul," Samson said solemnly. "Are you familiar with the story of Samson in the Bible?"

"I remember reading it as a kid."

"Then allow me to refresh your memory. My namesake was the mightiest Nazarite who ever lived. When the Spirit of the Lord came upon him, he was invincible. He slew a lion with his bare hands. He took on a Philistine army and killed a thousand of their soldiers—"

"Surely you don't take all of that literally," Andrew said, interrupting.

A scowl creased Samson's mouth. "I believe wholeheartedly in the Word of the Lord. If the Bible says that Samson defeated a thousand Philistines, then that's exactly what he did." He paused. "No one could best Samson until his Nazarite vow was violated. Delilah nagged him into revealing the secret of his strength, and the seven locks on his head were shaved off while he slept with his head resting on her knees. Thanks to her treachery, the Philistines were finally able to capture him. They put out his eyes, but they couldn't put out his passion for his Lord. Eventually his hair grew in again, and at a Philistine celebration where they were honoring their false god, Dagon, Samson took hold of the pillars supporting their temple and brought the building crashing down. He died true to his faith.''

"Are any of the other Warriors Nazarites?" Andrew inquired.

"I'm the only one."

Andrew looked at the man in blue. "What about you, Yama? What do you believe in?"

The silver-haired Warrior roused himself from his introspection and glanced at the farmer. "I believe in the Spirit, but my beliefs are different from Samson's. I attribute whatever strength I possess to the years I've spent building up my physique by weight lifting and daily strenuous exercise."

"Yama is unique among the Warriors," Samson said. "He is preoccupied with the subject of death."

"Have you been talking to Rikki?" Yama responded defensively. "I am *not* preoccupied with the subject of death."

"You took the name of the Hindu King of Death," Samson noted.

"True. But only because dealing in death is our business, our stock in trade. We're responsible for protecting everyone at the Home, and our responsibility entails eliminating anyone or anything that would harm those we love. Yama is a fitting name for someone who dispenses death for a living."

Samson nodded. "I agree with you there. But some of us think that you have carried the dispensing of death to an extreme."

"You're crazy," Yama snapped, and looked at the head Warrior. "You tell him, Blade. Tell him I don't go overboard."

"Don't get me involved in this," Blade replied, grinning.

Samson leaned toward his silver-haired companion. "There's no reason to be upset, brother. I'm not trying to insult you. Actually, I'm paying you a high compliment."

"You could have fooled me."

"I mean it. Of all the Warriors, you have achieved near perfection in your death-dealing skills," Samson said.

Yama's eyes narrowed. "What are you talking about? Many of the Warriors are more skilled than I am. Hickok, for instance, is a better shot with a revolver. Rikki-Tikki-Tavi is a better martial artist. Blade is better with a knife than I could ever hope to be. Teucer makes me look pitiful with a bow. And even in physical strength, you're stronger than I am.''

"You're missing the point," Samson said. "I'm not talking about individual skills. You are recognized as the best all-around Warrior in the Family. You have honed your skills to an exceptional degree. *All* of your skills, not just one or two. Yes, Hickok is a better shot, but only by a hair. Yes, Rikki is a better martial artist, but only by a shade. You've beaten him many times in sparring contests. And yes, Teucer can split a stick at one hundred yards with an arrow, but you can do the same feat at eighty yards. Of all the Warriors in the Family, you come closest to matching Blade's accomplishment with a knife.''

"What about you?''

"My physique has developed naturally. You've had to work diligently to perfect yours. And that's the key to your philosophy. You're a perfectionist. Your preoccupation with the techniques of dispensing death has made you the perfect Warrior.''

"Bull.''

"Suit yourself. But I know I'm right, and deep down in your heart, you do too.''

Yama snorted and resumed staring at the passing scenery.

"You know,'' Andrew said, turning to the giant, "you Warriors sure aren't anything like I would have expected.''

"How so?'' Blade asked without taking his eyes from the road.

"Well, after staying at the Home for two days, I got to know how your Family runs things. And quite frankly, I'm surprised that the Warriors are so different from one another. You were all raised in the same compound, or most of you were anyway. You were taught by the same Elders. You went through your Schooling years, as you refer to them, side by side in many cases. All of the Warriors had essentially the same childhood, and yet you're all so unlike each other.''

"Why should our differences surprise you?'' Blade responded. "Our differences are based on our personalities, not on our backgrounds. No two human personalities are ever alike, Andrew.''

"I've been meaning to tell you. Most folks call me Andy."

"All right, Andy. Are you hungry?" Blade questioned. He gazed upward through the windshield at the golden orb hovering at its zenith. "We can break out some venison jerky for lunch."

"We'd better hold off on the food," Yama advised.

"Why's that?" Blade asked, glancing over his right shoulder.

Yama nodded to the southeast. "We have suddenly become very popular."

Blade looked in the direction Yama had indicated and spied four leather-garbed figures on motorcycles. The riders were poised on a knoll 50 yards from the highway, and they were obviously watching the transport.

"There's more on this side," Samson declared.

Blade swiveled and discovered another eight or nine riders crossing a field, riding parallel to the road, keeping abreast of the SEAL. "This spells trouble," he stated.

"You don't know the half of it," Yama said, and pointed straight ahead.

A dozen motorcycles suddenly pulled out from the forest on both sides of the highway less than 70 yards from the van. They immediately formed a blockade across the road, and the riders quickly dismounted. A burly man in the middle took several steps and pointed a long object at the approaching transport.

Blade held off applying the brakes. He knew the SEAL's shatterproof body could withstand a bullet from any rifle. Then he peered intently at the long object, bothered by the unfamiliar contours of the weapon the biker held. For a second he thought the man might have a bazooka. Then recognition dawned and he stiffened.

The biker possessed a portable ground-to-ground missile launcher!

Chapter Five

Blade tramped on the brake pedal and brought the SEAL to a screeching halt. In his mind's eye he reviewed all of the books, magazines, and journals on military hardware that Kurt Carpenter had stocked in the Family library. He'd read every one, and he recalled a journal article on the state-of-the-art portable missile launchers in use at the time of World War Three. The weapon held by the burly biker was identical to a photograph in the journal. The man had a Dart, which fired a missile packing enough punch to knock out a tank. And the SEAL was the proverbial sitting duck.

"What are we going to do?" Andy asked nervously.

Blade glanced to the right and the left. The groups of riders on both sides were converging slowly on the transport. He studied their motorcycles, comparing the cycles to those used by a biker gang based in St. Louis known as the Leather Knights. He'd ridden on one of the mammoth machines driven by the Leather Knights. Hogs, he believed they were called. But these motorcycles weren't hogs. They were much smaller and sported thinner tires. What kind were they? he wondered.

"They're riding dirt bikes," Andy declared.

"Thanks," Blade said.

"For what?" Andrew asked as he picked up his rifle from the floor.

"Nothing," Blade replied. The man holding the Dart did not appear to be in any great hurry to fire the missile. Why not? Blade shifted his right foot from the brake to the accelerator and drove at under five miles an hour toward the bikers blocking the highway.

"What's your plan?" Yama asked.

"We'll play it be ear," Blade said.

"Why don't you just blow them to kingdom come?" Yama suggested. "You know what they want."

"We should try to save our rockets and missiles for the Technics," Blade stated. "There might be another way to take care of these clowns."

"I can take them out," Yama offered.

"Samson and you will stay put in the SEAL while I talk to them," Blade directed.

"You're not going to go out there alone?" Yama responded in disbelief.

"Yep."

"That's too risky. One of us should go with you."

"I agree with Yama," Samson chimed in. "You shouldn't go alone."

"You guys are worse than Hickok," Blade muttered, scrutinizing the bikers ahead. All of them were armed, either with a rifle, an assault rifle, or a machine gun. Most of them seemed to prefer black leather attire similar to the garments worn by the Leather Knights. Why did bikers have such a penchant for leather clothing?

"They must be scavengers," Andy opined, and looked at the giant. "If you step outside, they'll never let you climb back in."

Blade sighed and glanced at his fellow Warriors. "All right. Yama, you'll come with me."

"Why did you hesitate?" Yama inquired.

"I don't know what you're talking about," Blade told him, facing front.

"Yes, you do," Yama persisted. "It's not like you to be so indecisive. It's almost as if you don't trust us. Or one of us, anyway."

Samson turned toward his silver-haired friend. "I don't understand. Do you mean me?" he asked innocently.

"No. Me. Blade has his doubts about my reliability," Yama stated testily.

"I didn't say that," Blade declared.

"You didn't have to. I know you were reluctant to bring me on this run. You're worried I won't be able to pull my weight because of the way I feel about the Technics."

"How do you feel about the Technics?" Andy interjected.

"None of your business," Yama said.

"If I truly had grave doubts about your reliability, I wouldn't have brought you along," Blade said. "Yes, I'm worried about you. But I don't know if I'm more worried because of the Technics or the NDE you experienced in Seattle."

"What does my NDE have to do with this?" Yama queried.

"Everything. You've been behaving rather recklessly ever since," Blade said.

"What in the world is an NDE?" Andy inquired of no one in particular.

"Now is not the time to be discussing NDEs," Blade said. "We have more pressing concerns."

Yama eased to his left and bent forward, staring at Blade's profile. His forehead furrowed as he pondered the implications of his friend's unusual conduct. He recalled the incident in Seattle, marveling once again at the vivid memories the episode provoked. He had gone to the city, along with Blade, Hickok, and Rikki, to investigate the disappearance of a California Navy vessel. While fighting a vicious gang known as the Sharks, he'd taken an arrow in the back. Due to circumstances beyond their control, his companions had been unable to tend the wound and he had nearly bled to death. At one point, he'd experienced the strangest sensation of leaving his body, gliding through a mysterious tunnel, and entering a wonderful realm where peace and love reigned. He'd encountered a dazzling being of light, his inner Guide. And he'd seen—her—again.

Now, a year and a half later, he still hadn't come to complete terms with the Near Death Experience.

The NDE had changed him. Where before he had been quite naturally concerned about the prospect of his own demise and done everything in his power to prevent his passing, after the NDE he found his concerns obliterated. He couldn't worry about the possibility of dying if he *tried*. After all, of what consequence was death when he knew it was simply the method of passing from this life to the next, from the planet Earth to the higher mansions? He'd tried to explain his newfound perception to several of the other Warriors, but he discovered they were incapable of fully comprehending because they hadn't been through what he had been through.

How could an immortal explain the concept of eternal life to those who viewed themselves as mere mortals?

Yama gazed at Blade as the SEAL narrowed the gap to the bikers, reflecting. Perhaps he was being too hard on the giant. Blade wouldn't have agreed to bring him on the run if there were any serious doubts about his ability.

Unless . . .

Unless Blade had brought him along to test him, to evaluate his performance, to see if the NDE and his feelings about the Technics had made him *too* careless, too unstable for the post he held. Which would also explain Samson's presence. Blade had never taken Samson on a run before. Why now? Why on this trip to Green Bay? Blade knew that Samson and he were good friends. Had Blade brought Samson along to keep an eye on him? Would the head Warrior do such a thing? The notion angered him, and the anger provoked him even more. He prided himself on his consummate self-control. If he felt anger, then maybe Blade was right. Maybe he was unstable. He became aware of Blade speaking and shook his head to clear his thoughts.

" . . . eyes on the ones on the side of the highway."

"Will do," Samson replied.

"We'll leave the front windows rolled down. If we roll them up, the bikers might open fire," Blade said. He stopped the SEAL 20 yards from the bikers ahead and shifted into park. "Hand my guns to me, would you?"

Samson twisted in the seat and reached into the storage section comprising the rear third of the SEAL. Their supplies, ammunition, tools, and spare parts were piled high. Lying on top of the pile was a shoulder holster containing a Dan Wesson .44 Magnum and a Commando Arms Carbine. He grabbed the weapons and passed them to the giant.

"Thanks," Blade said. He placed the Commando between his legs and swiftly donned the shoulder holster, tucking the .44 Magnum under his left arm.

The four bikers on the right side of the road drew to within ten yards of the SEAL and stopped. They sat on their cycles, staring malevolently at the transport.

Blade looked to the left and saw the nine bikers on that side do the same. He lifted the Commando and glanced at the farmer.

Andrew had his Winchester in his lap, his finger on the trigger.

"Don't fire until I give the signal," Blade told him.

"I hope you know what you're doing," Andy said. "If it was up to me, I'd plow right through them."

Blade gestured at the biker armed with the Dart. "Do you see that missile launcher?"

"Is that what it is?"

"Yeah. And if that bozo fires, the SEAL will be blown to pieces. Do you still want me to try and plow through them?"

Andy gulped and shook his head. "Not really. We wouldn't want to do anything rash."

"When the shooting starts, duck down," Blade advised, and thrust his door open. He slid out with his back to the transport, warily surveying the bikers, ready to fire at the first hint of hostility, and pulled back the cocking handle on the Commando.

Samson slid into the driver's seat and poked his head out the window. "Be careful."

With a nod, Blade stepped to the front of the SEAL just as

Yama came around the passenger side.

The bikers blocking State Highway 46 kept the barrels of their weapons pointed at the ground.

"The guy with the Dart is mine," Blade whispered.

"Got you," Yama responded softly.

They advanced cautiously.

"Howdy!" called out the man holding the portable missile launcher. His fleshy round face split into a broad smile, but his cold brown eyes belied the friendly greeting. He wore a green shirt and faded jeans. "You are two of the biggest sons of bitches I've ever seen!"

Blade did not bother to respond. He halted eight yards from the row of bikers and slanted the Commando downward. One of his favorite weapons, converted to full automatic by the Family Gunsmiths, its original five-shot clip replaced by a 90-shot magazine, the Commando resembled the ancient Thompson submachine gun.

"My name is Bruno," the burly biker announced. "Who might you guys be?"

"What do you want?" Blade responded, ignoring the question. "Why have you blocked off the road?"

Bruno scowled. His right hand supported the Dart, which rested on his right shoulder, and his left hung by his side. "You're not being very polite, sucker."

"I'm just getting warmed up," Blade said contemptuously.

Bruno took a menacing stride forward. "You'd better watch your mouth, prick, or you're history."

"You plan to kill us one way or the other anyway, so what's the big deal?" Blade replied.

"Who says we're going to waste you?" Bruno asked. "All we want to do is talk."

Blade sighed and glanced at the skinny biker on the left who shifted nervously from foot to foot and repeatedly hefted an assault rifle, apparently eager to cut loose. "Don't play games with me, Bruno. I know what you're up to."

"Yeah?"

"Yeah," Blade said. "I've met your type before. You're a

scavenger. You make a living by taking what you want from those who rightfully own whatever you steal. You prey on anyone and everyone, and you've probably killed dozens of fine, innocent people. What you don't steal, you buy on the black market. Like that Dart, for instance. Where did you find your little toy?''

Bruno grinned slyly. ''You think you know it all, don't you, smart guy?''

''Where did you obtain the Dart?'' Blade asked, repeating his question.

''From the Armorer, a guy in Detroit who can supply any weapon you want if you can meet his price,'' Bruno disclosed, and eyed the missile launcher proudly. ''We traded him seven women for this baby.''

''Seven women?''

''Yeah. We hit a small town a while back and found seven foxes living there. They were real prime, if you get my drift.''

''You're disgusting,'' Blade remarked.

A belly laugh burst from the biker. ''Am I, now? Well, Mister Goody-Two-Shoes, if I'm such a bad cat, how come I didn't just blow you away the second I laid eyes on your van?''

''Because you want the van for yourself,'' Blade stated flatly. ''You don't want to destroy our vehicle if you can help it. So you set up this ambush, hoping to draw everyone inside out in the open where your buddies can gun them down.'' He paused. ''But your ploy hasn't worked. We have friends in there ready to take off if you open fire.''

Bruno snickered. ''And how far do you think they'd get? If I can't have your van, nobody can.''

''We've heard that line before,'' Blade said.

''Tough dudes, huh?'' Bruno commented, and chuckled. He gazed past the giant at the green van. ''Why can't I see inside that thing?''

''We have the curtains closed.''

''I've never seen a vehicle like yours,'' Bruno mentioned. ''I bet it'd be worth a ton of gold to the right party.''

''Like the Armorer?''

"Or the Commies. Or maybe even the Technics."

Blade tensed. "The Technics deal with the likes of you?"

"Up yours, mother," Bruno snapped, then added, "Yeah, they do. What of it? We keep them posted on everything we see and they fix our bikes for us and give us guns."

A convenient arrangement, Blade realized. The bikers served as eyes and ears for the Technics, an arrangement similar to the pact the Technics had worked out with the Leather Knights in St. Louis. The Technics weren't yet strong enough to subjugate the Midwest, so they maintained a spy network to keep them apprised of ongoing events. Crude, but effective.

"The Technics are all right," Bruno went on. "They treat us fairly. And they let us do whatever we want with the foxes we snatch." He paused. "You got any foxes in that van?"

"No," Blade said.

"Too bad," Bruno stated. "I could go for some fluff. We might even let you live if you had some women for us." He snorted. "Except for those Technic bitches. I had one once. Boy, was she lame in the sack. Those Technics can't screw for beans."

Blade felt his abdominal muscles tighten.

"Yes, sir. I could go for a little fuzz right about now," Bruno said. He was surprised when the other guy, the one in blue who hadn't spoken a word, suddenly took a step toward him.

"How about a little lead instead?" Yama asked, and before any of the bikers could hope to react to his threat, he leveled the Wilkinson and fired.

Chapter Six

It took three and a half seconds for the startled bikers to react to the sudden attack, and in the brief span the silver-haired Warrior downed six of the bikers. He whipped the Wilkinson barrel in a tight arc and sent a withering hail of bullets into the scavengers. His first rounds ripped into the fleshy features of the scavenger leader, tearing Bruno's face to shreds. Several of the bikers screamed as they died.

Blade had intuitively sensed, a fraction of an instant before Yama squeezed the trigger, that the man in blue was about to wade into the gang. He brought the Commando barrel up with a flick of his wrist and added his firepower to Yama's, going for the scavengers directly in front of him, the louder blasting of the Commando drowning out all other noise. He felt the short hairs at the nape of his neck tingle, and he wondered if one of the bikers on the side of the road would shoot him before he could whirl to confront them. He saw two scavengers hurled to the asphalt, their torsos perforated and gushing crimson, then three, four, five of them were dead or dying, leaving a tall biker who was taking a bead on his chest with a rifle. Blade started to throw himself to the left, knowing the man would fire before he could leap out of the way.

Several rounds suddenly bored into the scavenger's forehead and catapulted him backwards.

Blade spun, crouching as he did, sweeping the Commando at the nine bikers to the left of the highway, but someone had already beaten him to them.

Samson had both his steely arms sticking out of the window on the driver's side, and in each malletlike hand he held a Bushmaster Auto Pistol. At a range of ten yards he had emptied both 30-shot magazines into the scavengers on his side of the road. Two of them had managed to get off wild shots that struck the SEAL and ricocheted off. Now six of the nine were prone on the ground, their motorcycles lying beside them or under them, while two others had fallen to their knees and were aiming at the Nazarite.

Blade disposed of the duo with a short burst, then scanned the field for the last of the nine. Twenty yards to the north, and rapidly gaining speed, was a wounded biker who weaved unsteadily, struggling to control the handlebars on his machine. Blade took three quick, long strides, pressed the stock to his right shoulder, and stitched a straight pattern of red dots down the middle of the scavenger's back.

The biker flung his arms wide and toppled from his cycle, which continued to wobble for a good ten yards before it crashed onto its side.

Blade pivoted, anxious about the four bikers on the right side of the highway. Two of the four were sprawled on the grass, and the remaining pair were fleeing for their lives, their engines revved to the maximum, racing to the south.

Yama materialized at the edge of Highway 46, the Wilkinson slung over his left shoulder. He drew the Smith and Wesson and clasped the gun in his right hand while bracing his wrist with his left. Exercising deliberate care, he sighted on the lead biker and fired. The gun boomed, and 30 yards away the scavenger tumbled to the turf, flipping off the back of his bike and landing on his head. His cycle veered toward the last biker, causing the man to angle sharply to the right. Yama aimed and slowly squeezed the trigger, and he displayed no emotion when his shot caught the man between the shoulder blades. Both the biker and the bike fell over.

Blade surveyed the carnage, verifying that all of the scavengers were out of commision. Some were groaning or whining pitiably, but none were in any condition to continue the fight. He walked over to Yama and motioned at the slain leader. "What the hell did you think you were doing?"

"Eliminating the enemy before they could eliminate us," Yama responded stiffly. He began to reload the Smith and Wesson.

"I didn't give the signal to open fire," Blade said angrily.

"I jumped the gun."

"You're damn right you did. And do you know why?"

Yama studiously avoided his friend's gaze. He palmed a spent cartridge and shrugged. "I felt it was necessary."

"And I feel it's necessary to put you on report. If you don't shape up, you'll find yourself in front of a Review Board when we return to the Home."

Yama looked down at the ground.

"I want you to check each and every biker. Put every one who isn't dead out of his misery," Blade ordered.

"Right away," Yama said softly, and walked off.

Blade sighed and moved toward the SEAL, annoyed at himself. He'd brought Yama along against his better judgment, and he shouldn't have. He knew how devastated Yama had been after her death. So how could he blame the man for doing what he would have done under the same circumstances?

Samson stepped into view next to the right front tire, holding his Bushmaster Auto Rifle, his features downcast.

"Did you see what happened?" Blade asked.

"I saw."

"We were lucky the scavengers were sloppy. Yama's blunder would have cost us dearly if they'd been real pros. So cheer up. It could have been a lot worse."

"It is," Samson said.

"What?" Blade responded, and from the look in Samson's eyes he immediately perceived the Nazarite's meaning. "Oh, no.''

"I'm afraid so," Samson stated.

Blade hurried to the window on the passenger side and peered inside, sadness overcoming him. He slapped the SEAL in frustration.

A bullet had struck Andrew Wolksi on the bridge of the nose and drilled through his cranium, splattering blood and brains over the console and the dash. He lay on his back on the console, his lifeless eyes fixed on the roof, his mouth hanging slack and his tongue protruding.

Dear Spirit, no!

Blade closed his eyes and bowed his head. Not him! The farmer had gone to so much effort to locate the Family, to secure aid for his wife and daughter, and now Andy would never see them again in this life. He heard footsteps and glanced up.

"He didn't duck as you told him to do," Samson said, coming to the window. "He tried to fight and shot one of them. Then he got hit."

"We'll have to bury him here," Blade stated. "I'm not about to leave his body for the buzzards and the mutants. He deserves a proper burial." Scowling, he slung the Commando over his left arm.

Samson nodded, then reached up and rubbed his right hand on his neck. When he removed the hand, blood streaked his fingers.

"You were hit too," Blade declared. He bent closer and examined the Nazarite's neck. A bullet had carved a fine groove, just breaking the skin, and a trickle of blood seeped from the torn flesh.

"It's just a scratch," Samson responded. "The shot that killed Andy went clear through him and struck me. If I'd been several more inches to the right, I'd be lying in there with him."

"Get the first-aid kit and I'll clean it for you," Blade offered.

"I'm fine. Really."

"What is this? Doesn't anyone here know how to listen? Go get the damn first-aid kit."

"Yes, sir," Samson replied, and extended his right arm to

grab the door handle. He hesitated, realizing he would have to crawl over Andrew to reach the storage section, then headed for the other side. "Be back in a jiffy."

Blade heard the burp of Yama's Wilkinson. He walked to the front of the transport and watched the man in blue finish off the scavengers. What now? he asked himself. Should they turn around and return to the Home? Did Wolski's death have any bearing on their mission? No, he decided. Even though rescuing Sandra and Nadine had been Andrew's overriding concern, and even though Blade would do everything in his power to locate and save them, of more critical consequence to the Family were the Technic activities in Green Bay. If the Technics were up to their usual dirty tricks, they had to be stopped. Proceeding with the mission was imperative.

Which left him with the problem of what to do about Yama.

Blade observed the man in blue walk over to a prone scavenger who had a half-dozen bullet holes in his back, but who was still alive, moaning and sobbing. Yama placed the Wilkinson barrel against the base of the biker's skull and fired. The scavenger convulsed for a few seconds, then lay still. With methodical precision, Yama continued on his circuit.

What a shame.

Blade had always rated the man in blue as one of the best Warriors and considered Yama to be extremely dependable. But after the death of the Technic woman, Yama had changed. Not outwardly, not in any obvious manner, but to his close friends the change had been noticeable, a slight lessening of his zest for life. Where before Yama had thrown himself into his craft with a fiery passion, after Alicia Farrow's death he had seemed to lose some of his emotional zeal. He went through all the motions, practiced as diligently as ever, but some of his inner spark had burned out.

Until the Near Death Experience.

No one could quite figure out why the NDE had so totally transformed Yama's personality. While Blade had rejoiced to see Yama filled with fire again, he'd been disturbed by the way Yama waded into battle with a bewildering, reckless abandon.

Talk about being careless.

After experiencing the NDE, Yama seemed to view himself as invulnerable. No matter the odds against him, he didn't care. He would fight any number of enemies, head-on. And where before he had fought with supreme skill, now he added to his skill an arrogant attitude, an air of presumed invincibility that potentially threatened not only his life, but the lives of the Warriors he worked with.

Blade had hoped that the silver-haired Warrior had adjusted to the loss of Alicia Farrow and the Near Death Experience, but quite obviously Yama had not. One of the best Warriors now lacked the single most important attribute: self-control. And without self-control, it would only be a matter of time before Yama's recklessness brought about his undoing.

What a rotten shame.

Yama approached, the Wilkinson slung over his right shoulder. "All of the scavengers are dead."

"Have you looked inside the SEAL yet?" Blade asked.

"No. Should I?"

"Yes," Blade stated harshly.

Yama's brow knit at the tone his friend used. He pivoted and hastened to the door on the passenger side.

"Here's the first-aid kit," Samson announced, coming up behind the giant.

Blade turned and took the kit. He knelt, flipped up the lid, and found gauze and a bottle of hydrogen peroxide. The bottle had come from a shipment of supplies received in trade with the Civilized Zone.

"I gather we'll continue to Green Bay," Samson remarked.

"Yep."

"What will we do with Andrew's wife and daughter if we find them?"

"Whatever they want. We'll take them to their relatives, or they can come live at the Home," Blade responded gruffly. He opened the bottle, grabbed the gauze in his other hand, and stood.

"Something is bothering you, my brother," Samson observed.

"What do you think is bothering me?"

"Yama?"

"Bingo."

"Trust in the Lord," Samson said. "Everything will work out."

Blade nodded absently and proceeded to clean the bullet wound. The trickle of blood had ceased, enabling him to complete the cleaning quickly. He replaced the gauze and the hydrogen peroxide in the kit and took out a box of bandages.

"I won't need a bandage," Samson stated. "My mother always told me that injuries heal faster when they're exposed to the air."

"Suit yourself," Blade said. He stuck the bandages in the kit and closed the lid. "Would you put this back in the SEAL?"

Samson took the first-aid kit and walked off.

"And bring the shovel too," Blade added. He saw the Nazarite's head bob up and down. Girding himself for the distasteful task, he moved to the passenger side and stopped in surprise when his gaze fell on Yama.

The silver-haired Warrior stood with his head bowed, his hands gripping the lower edge of the window, and his eyes closed. His features were a study in misery.

Blade slowly stepped up to the door.

"I'm responsible for his death, aren't I?" Yama asked without opening his eyes.

"More or less," Blade admitted.

"I never wanted Andrew to be harmed. You know that, don't you?"

"Yes."

"I didn't want to lose control."

"I know."

"But when that bastard started insulting Technic women, I kept thinking of her, of the happiness we shared," Yama said, and his next words were strained and barely audible. "I've never loved any woman but her.''

"I know."

Yama looked up, his haunted eyes conveying his inner turmoil. "Why, Blade? Why is it all coming to the surface now? It's been three years!"

"Let me ask you a question."

"Anything."

"What did you do the day after she died?''

Yama blinked a few times, as if the query had been completely unexpected. "I worked the next day. Wall duty, I believe. Why?"

"And the night she was killed?"

"You know what happened. She betrayed the Technics and gave her life to spare mine."

"That's not what I meant," Blade said. "Did you cry on the night she died?"

"A little," Yama replied in a whisper.

"Then is it any wonder that you can't control your emotions where the Technics are involved? For three years you've been simmering under the surface like an overheated pot ready to boil over. You lost the only woman you've loved, and you never came to grips with that loss. You never let your emotions out,'' Blade stated, and placed his right hand on Yama's shoulder. "Even when a person believes in the Spirit, as we do, and even when we know that those who die pass on to the higher mansions, the loss of a loved one can be a terrible experience. If we try to suppress our emotions and keep all our hurt and anguish inside, eventually we'll explode."

"So how do I let it out? I've practiced total self-control for so long, I don't know if I *can* let it out."

"You must find a way," Blade told him. "If you don't, if you can't stem your erratic behavior, then your days as a Warrior are numbered."

Chapter Seven

"What's our approximate location?" Blade asked.

Samson consulted the map in his lap, running his finger along the route they were following. "I estimate we're a quarter of a mile west of New London."

"And how far is it from New London to Green Bay?"

"I'd say about thirty-five miles, give or take a few," Samson responded. He glanced out his open window at the trees flashing by and shifted in the bucket seat. "We'll be there soon."

"We've made good time," Blade commented. A day and a half had elapsed since the incident involving the bikers, a day and a half during which Yama had barely spoken a word. Blade glanced over his right shoulder at the man in blue, who sat behind Samson. "How's it going back there?"

"Just peachy," Yama responded sullenly. His right elbow was propped on his leg, his chin in his hand, the picture of gloom.

Blade wished he could say something—anything—to soothe his friend's melancholic soul. If Yama didn't snap out of his depression before they tangled with the Technics, he might never be afforded the opportunity to recover.

"Will we go around New London?" Samson inquired.

Blade nodded. Prior experience had taught him the prudence

of bypassing every city and town on the map. The gangs, raiders, and scavengers tended to congregate in or near the inhabited centers, although they could be encountered anywhere. And even in those towns still under the control of generally peaceable residents, the citizens were often inclined to greet strangers by shooting first and questioning intent second. So although the runs invariably took much longer because of the practice, Blade insisted on skirting cities and towns wherever possible.

"Will we try to locate Andrew's farm?" Samson queried.

"What good would it do? No one is living there now."

"We could look for one of his neighbors and get the latest information on the Technics," Samson suggested.

"Is it wise to advertise our presence?" Blade responded. "For all we know, the neighbor might run into Green Bay and inform the Technics that we're here. I'd rather surprise them. We'll hide the SEAL on the outskirts of the city and go in tonight. Under the cover of darkness we should be able to sneak right up to the University of Wisconsin and see for ourselves what's going on."

"Fine by me."

Blade spotted a field on the right side of the highway and angled the transport off the road. Its huge tires crushed all the weeds and brush in their path. He crossed the field and entered a belt of woods, skillfully threading a course among the trees. Once the transport spooked a buck and two does from a dense thicket and they bounded away with their white tails upraised.

Ten minutes went by.

"We should be well past New London by now," Blade commented, and slanted their path to the north and the highway. The SEAL emerged from the forest at a curve in the road. Nearby, still legible after so many years, stood a sign stating they were on State Highway 54.

Blade increased speed, pushing the SEAL as fast as the road conditions warranted. He wanted to reach Green Bay before nightfall so they would have plenty of time to conceal the van. Thoughts of Jenny and Gabe brought a smile to his lips. He looked forward to completing the assignment and returning to the Home. Being away from his loved ones for even a short spell made him homesick.

"Thinking of your better half?" Samson unexpectedly asked.

Blade glanced at the Nazarite. "Are you psychic?"

"No, but I was thinking of Naomi, Benjamin, and Ruth, and I smiled at the same moment you did. Just a lucky guess," Samson said.

"How did they take your leaving on this run?"

"They weren't overjoyed about it, but they know that my duties as a Warrior require that we make certain sacrifices from time to time," Samson answered. Am impish twinkle came into his eyes and he cleared his throat. "By the way, I heard about the conversation between Jenny and Naomi. I was rather surprised to hear the news."

"What news?" Blade asked idly.

"About Jenny and you trying for another child soon," Samson said. He had to repress a laugh when the giant clenched the steering wheel tightly and did a remarkable imitation of a stranded fish gulping air.

"Another child?" Blade blurted out, stunned by the revelation. "Jenny wants another baby?"

"So she told Naomi. She's getting the urge, as she put it," Samson elaborated.

A frustrated grunt issued from Blade's throat. "Jenny hasn't said a word to me."

"Maybe she's hoping to surprise you," Samson mentioned.

"Some surprise," Blade muttered.

"Well, you know how women are."

"Boy, don't I." Blade shook his head in astonishment. "Why don't wives ever come right out in the open with what's on their minds? Why do husbands always have to pry the information out of them with a crowbar?"

"It's traditional, I believe."

Blade snorted. "How do you figure?"

"Haven't you heard? Husbands are always the last to know."

"If you ask me—" Blade began, then checked his statement

when he spied the wagon on the highway several hundred yards off. He slowed and leaned forward.

"Dear Lord!" Samson exclaimed.

The wooden wagon partly obstructed the road. Lying in front of it, still attached to their harnesses, were the carcasses of two horses. Several bodies were lying on the ground close by. And perched on the corpses or standing about them, flapping their wings and pecking at the putrid flesh, were a score of large black birds distinguished by bare, reddish necks and heads.

"Are those turkey vultures?" Samson asked.

"Yes," Blade replied, and floored the accelerator, reducing the distance rapidly. A few of the vultures took to the air, but the rest of the flock stubbornly feasted until the transport was almost upon them. Then, in a swirling, fluttering mass, they swooped into the air and rose high above the highway. Blade braked, put the SEAL in park, and grabbed the Commando from the console. "Let's go," he said, and opened his door.

The turkey vultures were circling far overhead.

Cradling his Commando, Blade dropped to the cracked asphalt and walked toward the wagon. A revolting stench assailed his nostrils and he almost gagged. He covered his nose with his left hand and walked to within a few yards of the first body.

Samson and Yama joined him.

"What could have caused *this*?" Samson exclaimed, aghast.

"I don't know," Blade replied, his eyes on the two men and one woman.

All three of the bodies had been, quite literally, torn to pieces. Heads were severed from necks. Arms and legs were lying inches from the forms to which they had been attached. One of the victims, a man in his fifties, had sustained a split skull. The woman lay on her back, a homespun dress pulled up around her breasts, her stringy intestines piled on her ruptured abdomen.

Yama stepped over to the woman and studied her remains, his countenance clinically inscrutable. "There aren't any claw marks. I doubt animals were responsible."

"What then?" Samson asked. "A mutation of some kind?"

Blade moved to the wagon and discovered three battered suitcases in the bed. None of the suitcases had been opened, which eliminated robbery as a motive. If scavengers had been the culprits, the contents would have been scattered all over and everything of value would be missing.

Yama turned his attention to the dead horses. Both were intact, but their heads were horribly swollen and discolored. "These horses were beaten to death," he announced. "There are multiple contusions around the eyes and ears."

"Any teeth or claw marks at all?" Blade inquired.

"None," Yama replied.

Blade gazed to the east, the direction from which the wagon had been heading when the occupants were overtaken by their grisly fate. Did the hapless trio hail from Green Bay?

"Did you see these suitcases?" Samson asked while looking into the wagon bed.

"Yeah," Blade answered thoughtfully.

"Maybe they were taking a trip or a vacation," the Nazarite speculated.

"Or maybe they were fleeing for their lives," Blade said, "and whatever they were fleeing caught up with them."

Yama walked over to the wagon. He glanced at the suitcases, then the corpses. "I'd guess they were killed sometime last night, between midnight and three A.M."

Blade nodded, pleased that the man in blue had temporarily shaken off his doleful mood. "And whatever killed them might still be in the area. Let's get in the SEAL and keep going."

They returned to the transport, climbed inside, and a minute later were en route once again to Green Bay. They sat in silence, reflecting on the horror they had witnessed. Shortly another town appeared directly ahead, a small hamlet named Shiocton, which Blade skirted.

"Twenty-four miles to Green Bay," Samson declared when they were again on Highway 54 and driving eastward.

"How far to Seymour, the town Wolski lived near?" Blade asked.

"In less than six miles there will be a turnoff on the left. If you took that for a mile or so, you'd reach Seymour.''

"We'll stick to this highway," Blade said. "Barring unforeseen complications, we should be at Green Bay within the
hour.''

"And how far to the Indian reservation?'' Yama threw in.

Samson shrugged. "Oh, about six and a half miles tops, if
our map is accurate.''

"It's been accurate so far,'' Blade remarked. He spotted the
roofs of two structures visible above the trees on his side of
the road and judged the buildings to be situated 50 yards from
the highway. A farm or ranch, he reasoned, and did not bother
to let up on the accelerator. If they were to make Green Bay
before nightfall, they couldn't afford any distractions. He
inadvertently yawned, covering his mouth with his left hand.

"Look!'' Samson cried, and pointed at Highway 54.

Blade almost missed the sight. He stopped yawning and stared
ahead, and there was a young woman attired in jeans and a torn
brown blouse dashing across the road from south to north, her
long brunette hair flying. He stuck his head out and yelled,
"Hey! We won't hurt you!'' But she had already crossed the
road and vanished in the forest.

"Do we go after her?'' Samson inquired.

"One of us does,'' Blade said as he applied the brakes.
"Yama, go get her. We'll wait for you. Don't take long. I want
to question her and take off right away for Green Bay.''

"Roger,'' Yama responded, scooping up the Wilkinson from
the seat. The instant the SEAL stopped, he was out of the door
and racing in pursuit of the woman. In seconds the undergrowth
swallowed him up.

"Shouldn't we go with him?'' Samson asked.

"I don't want to leave the SEAL unattended on the highway,''
Blade replied. "Yama can handle her.''

The Nazarite studied the giant for a moment. "Very shrewd,
if I do say so myself.''

"What are you talking about?''

"By letting Yama go after her alone, you're demonstrating
to him that you have confidence in his ability. And by giving

him something to do, you're helping him to get his mind off his problems," Samson said. "I never quite realized how tactful you are."

"I try."

They waited expectantly for their silver-haired friend to return.

"I never got around to thanking you properly for bringing me on this mission," Samson commented after a bit.

"You're welcome."

"Why me, Blade?"

"Haven't you heard? I've implemented a new policy. I plan to take Warriors who don't have extensive combat experience on more assignments in the future."

Samson draped his left arm on the console. "I know about the policy you implemented after your return from Boston. But are you sure there wasn't another reason you brought me along on this particular mission?"

Blade glanced at the Nazarite. He hadn't bothered to tell Samson his ulterior motive because he had wanted to avoid possibly embarrassing Yama. And too, he'd never expected Samson to ascertain the truth. He had to remind himself that underneath all those bulging muscles was a mind as keen as his own. "There was another reason," he confessed.

"I figured as much."

"I was hoping you would help keep an eye on Yama."

Samson stared at the point where Yama had entered the forest. "Why didn't you come right out and tell me?"

"I should have. I apologize," Blade said. He drummed his fingers on the steering wheel, his eyes glued to the forest. Yama should be returning soon, he told himself. He knew how fast Yama could move, and he doubted the woman they'd seen would be able to outdistance the fleet-footed Warrior. In just a few minutes Yama would be back with the woman in tow.

The time seemed to drag by.

"Maybe I should go look for him?" Samson proposed five minutes later.

"No."

''What if he's in trouble?''

''Yama can take care of himself. Besides, we'd hear gunfire if he ran into any serious opposition.''

''You hope.''

The corners of Blade's mouth curved down and he scanned the woods for any movement. All he saw was a robin and a butterfly. His impatience mounted as the minutes ticked past. He wondered if he had made another mistake, and if he should drive the SEAL into the forest, camouflaging the transport with broken limbs and brush, then search for Yama. Engrossed in his deliberations, he didn't hear the approaching vehicle until Samson suddenly poked him in the shoulder.

''Behind us!''

Blade turned, his gray eyes widening when he saw the four soldiers wearing dark green uniforms who were riding in a topless jeep. He recognized those distinctive uniforms instantly.

Technics!

Only 30 yards away and closing rapidly!

Chapter Eight

Yama raced through the forest with all the swiftness and stealth of a mountain lion, effortlessly vaulting obstacles in his path such as downed trees and small boulders. He ran around a thicket and glimpsed the woman far ahead, angling to the east. Her speed impressed him. She moved as someone who was accustomed to the terrain. He sped after her, his legs pumping.

The brunette came to the crest of a low rise and paused to look over her right shoulder. She spotted the man in blue and promptly plunged ahead.

Yama held the Wilkinson in his left hand. He could feel the scimitar swaying on his thigh. A pine tree loomed in front of him and he swung past it on the right. When he reached the rise, he stopped, getting his bearings.

Still fleeing with the surefootedness of a deer, the brunette was heading in the direction of several structures visible through the trees.

Yama sped after her. Those were the same buildings partly observable from the highway. He speculated that she might be making for her home, where she could elicit the aid of her family. The trees thinned the farther he went, and in a minute they gave way entirely to a wide field. Beyond the field were a farmhouse, a red barn, and a shed.

The woman had already covered three fourths of the distance. Boy, could she ever move!

With a flat stretch in front of him, Yama went all out. Of all the Warriors, only Rikki-Tikki-Tavi, Blade and Spartacus—once—had ever bested him in a foot race. And had they been with him there, they would have been hard-pressed to match his lightning pace. With his arms and legs flying, he seemed to flow over the ground, and he quickly narrowed the brunette's lead.

She came to the edge of the meticulously trimmed yard and looked at her pursuer again, then bolted for the three-story white farmhouse. To the north of the house stood the barn. The brown shed was situated between the two, only a dozen yards from the rear of the farmhouse.

No one else was in sight.

Yama gripped the Wilkinson with both hands and scrutinized the buildings carefully. He was approaching from the south-west, and the house, shed, and barn all fronted to the south. A gravel drive led from the farmhouse toward the highway.

The brunette ran to the front of the farmhouse and dashed inside.

Wary of being shot at from one of the windows, Yama slowed, his eyes flicking from pane to pane, the Wilkinson trained upward. He crossed the yard quickly, puzzled by the lack of activity in the house. If there were people living inside, surely one of them would challenge him. Or were they hiding, afraid he would slay them? He stayed far enough from the farm-house to keep every window on the side he approached within his field of view.

No one appeared.

The front door hung slightly open. He started toward it, then stopped abruptly when he spied the black form lying in the grass 15 yards to the east of the home. A hairy leg, resembling a bent stick, projected a foot and a half into the air.

A dog?

Yama cautiously advanced toward the form, his eyes narrowing when he saw the blood-spattered body clearly. The canine turned out to be a dead collie, its head transformed into a crimson pulp. Right away he remembered the dead horses, and he wondered if there might be a correlation. But why would anyone go around beating horses and dogs to death? And if the animals had been slain by whoever—or whatever—had killed those three people in the wagon, why were only the people torn apart?

A muffled crash sounded inside the farmhouse.

Pivoting, Yama darted to the entrance and kicked the door wide. He scanned a long hallway, then eased over the threshold with his back pressed firmly against the right-hand wall. There were three doorways on the right, two on the left, and he went from one to the other, searching the rooms he found: a living room, a dining room, a spacious kitchen in which a wood-burning stove squatted in the middle of the tiled floor, and a sewing room containing an antique sewing machine. When he opened the last door on the right, his finger caressing the Wilksinson's trigger, he smiled at the sight of a narrow flight of stairs leading to the upper floors.

Had the brunette taken refuge upstairs?

Yama ascended hastily, well aware his friends would be anxiously awaiting his return. On the second floor he discovered three bedrooms and a bath.

But no brunette.

He walked to a closed door at the end of the hall. A sharp twist of his left wrist and a brisk tug sufficed to disclose another flight of stairs. These were even narrower than the first flight, with barely enough room for a person to walk comfortably. At the top, ten steps up, an open door framed a patch of sunlight that apparently streamed in from a nearby window.

An attic maybe?

Yama started toward the sunlight. On the fifth step he abruptly halted, listening to the crackle of gunfire in the distance, from the direction of the highway and the SEAL.

Blade and Samson!

Without considering his personal safety, he wheeled, about to bound down the stairs and race to the aid of his companions.

As he spun, out of the corner of his right eye he detected a shadow materializing in the doorway above. He tried to reverse his spin, but something heavy slammed into his right shoulder and knocked him from his feet, upending him, and he somersaulted out of control onto the hard floor below, landing on his left side. The jarring impact racked his ribs with an intense spasm of excruciating pain, doubling him over and causing him to inadvertently release the Wilkinson. Through the haze of agony he heard something clatter onto the floor, then the patter of rushing feet. He places his right hand on the floor and tried to push erect, surprised at the degree of pain he felt, surmising he must have jammed his ribs on the carbine's stock.

The Wilkinson!

Yama reached his knees, but someone else beat him to the weapon.

"Don't move!" the brunette ordered. She was standing near the stairs, the Wilkinson clenched firmly in her slim hands, her green eyes ablaze with hatred. Dirt and grime streaked her pear-shaped face. Her brown blouse had been torn on the left side from the bottom hem almost to her arm. Mud spots dotted her jeans and her brown leather shoes. Her disheveled hair hung to her shoulder blades. Within inches of her feet lay a large, overturned toolbox.

Yama froze, straining his ears to catch the sound of gunshots, but all he heard was her heavy breathing.

"I've got you, you murdering son of a bitch!" she snapped. "And now I'm going to make you pay!"

"I'm not who you think I am," Yama informed her.

"Shut your face!" she growled, and took a menacing stride toward him. "Don't tempt me to pull this trigger, because by God I will!"

"I believe you," Yama said, his mind racing. How could he get out of this fix? His friends might be in desperate need of assistance. He had to disarm her, and swiftly. His ribs were already beginning to feel better. If only he could draw her closer. "What's your name?"

"Why the hell should you care?" the brunette responded bitterly. "All you're interested in is seeing me dead."

"That's not true."

Her face became a livid red. "Liar!" she exploded. "All of you Technics are rotten, filthy liars!"

Yama looked her in the eyes. "I'm not a Technic."

An acidic, mocking laugh burst from her lips. "Sure you're not. I suppose you're a farmer!"

"I'm a Warrior."

She cocked her head and scrutinized him closely.

"Do I look like a Technic?" Yama asked her. "Am I wearing the kind of clothes a Technic would wear? You saw the van I came here in. Is that the kind of vehicle the Technics use?"

The corners of her eyes crinkled, betraying her incipient doubt. "If you're not a Technic, why were you chasing me?"

"The man who heads the Warriors wants to talk to you."

"I'll bet he does," she said sarcastically, then glanced at the revolver and pistol. "All right, bastard. Place your guns on the floor and do it very slowly."

"You're making a mistake," Yama advised her.

"No, *you* made the mistake, you and the rest of your Technic buddies, when you had my dad, mom, and brother murdered! But those things didn't get me. My dad told me to run, told me he would hold them off, and my brother shoved me into the woods. I tried to go back, but it was all over in—" she stated, and her voice broke as tears moistened her eyes.

Taking advantage of the opportunity, Yama began to rise.

"Don't!" she screamed, waving the Wilkinson wildly. "Stay put or else!"

Yama sank down and sighed.

"I'm going to alert the whole countryside to what you're up to," the brunette declared. "Somehow, some way, you'll be stopped. Those things will be wiped out."

"What things?"

"Don't play innocent with me," she admonished him. "You know what things I'm talking about. Those poor people that the Mad Scientist changed into . . . the walking dead."

"These walking dead killed your family?"

"You know they did!" the brunette responded angrily. "Now do as I told you. Put your guns on the floor."

Yama hesitated. He wanted to rejoin Blade and Samson, and he wouldn't be able to leave until he gained the upper hand. Jumping her was an option, and although he felt confident he could reach her before she shot him, he opted to try a different tack. "No," he replied.

"What?" she asked, startled.

"I'm not putting my guns on the floor. I'm going to stand up, slowly, and leave."

"You'll do no such thing."

"I can't stay here any longer," Yama said. "My friends are in trouble and I must go to them."

"I'll shoot."

"Have you ever shot anyone before?"

Uncertainty crept into her countenance and she shook her head. "But there's always a first time."

"Believe me, you don't want to kill another person if you can possibly avoid it. Killing changes you, marks you for life, sets you apart from almost everyone else."

She started at him, obviously bewildered. "Strange words coming from a Technic."

"I'm not a Technic," Yama reiterated, and straightened, holding his arms out from his sides to demonstrate his peaceful intent.

"Don't!"

"You can come with me if you desire," Yama said.

Her green eyes flashed. "You're not going anywhere, damn you."

Taking a calculated gamble, the Warrior took a step backwards. "I mean you no harm."

"I'm warning you," she said, pointing the Wilkinson at his midriff.

"You can keep the carbine if you want," Yama commented, and took another step.

"Please don't force me to shoot you," she said, her voice wavering.

"I don't believe you'll fire."

"You're wrong," she assured him.

"Am I?" Yama countered, then tensed when a metallic crash arose from downstairs.

The brunette started in alarm and gazed past him at the stairway to the ground floor. "What was that?" she whispered.

"How should I know?" Yama said.

"Don't talk so loud," she cautioned. "It could be them."

"Who?"

"The *things,*" she said, and licked her lips. "They used to only come out at night, but now they hunt in the daytime too."

"Let's go see," Yama suggested.

"Don't be crazy," she stated, her forehead creasing, gazing at him in transparent confusion.

Yama listened to more noise, to clanging and banging and loud pounding, and he deduced there must be someone throwing pots and pans around in the kitchen. "I'll be back in a bit," he said, and took a pace.

"No!" the brunette exclaimed, coming closer, the Wilkinson dipping half a foot.

"Make up your mind, would you? First you're all set to blow me away, and now you're afraid I'll be killed. Which do you want?"

She uttered a strangled whine indicative of the turbulent state of her mind, her lips compressing. "I don't know!" she hissed. "But don't go downstairs."

"I have to," Yama stated, and turned to leave.

"Please!" she blurted out, stepping after him, her left arm reaching out to grab his wrist.

Which was the opening for which he'd been waiting. Yama whirled, his right hand streaking to the Wilkinson, and wrenched the weapon from her grasp.

She turned into a statue, too frightened to twitch a finger, her wide eyes on the carbine, her breath caught in her throat.

"Stay put while I investigate," Yama directed.

The racket in the kitchen had grown progressively louder, as if there were more than one person involved in producing the clamor.

"Aren't you going to shoot me?" she queried tremulously.

"I have this standard policy. I never shoot bunny rabbits and damsels in distress. Now if you'll excuse me," Yama said, but before he could move the din downstairs suddenly ceased.

"Dear God!" the brunette breathed, staring at the stairs.

Yama heard it too.

The pounding of heavy boots on the steps.

Chapter Nine

Blade placed his left arm on the window, drew the .44 Magnum, nestled the barrel under his arm pointing outward, and cocked the hammer. He looked into the side mirror, watching the uncoming jeep, and saw the driver slant the vehicle toward his side of the SEAL. "Slip out your door," he ordered Samson. "Cue on me."

"May the Lord guide your hands," the Nazarite said. He cracked the passenger door, then slid to the ground.

Plastering a friendly smile on his face, Blade glanced down as the jeep coasted to a stop alongside the transport.

A tall man sporting silver insignia on his lapels stared suspiciously at the Warrior. Lying in his lap was one of the distinctive assault rifles specifically manufactured by the Technics for their troops, a Dakon II. The entire weapon, including the folding stock and the 20-inch barrel, was black to reduce reflection. A short silencer suppressed each shot, and a 30-shot magazine provided ample rounds. Mounted above the ejection chamber was an elaborate scope, and atop the scope at the front end projected a four-inch tube capable of generating a red beam of light, a targeting laser used to pinpoint foes with astounding accuracy. A button on top of the scope activated the Laser Sighting Mode. There were four other buttons, located on the stock on the right side, and a small digital display above them. The digital readout kept track of the number of rounds expended and would light up when the first button was pressed. The second button put the Dakon in full automatic, the third semiautomatic, and the fourth ejected spent magazines.

Blade knew the weapon well. He had used one extensively during his last run-in with the Technics. "Hi there," he greeted the officer. "Can I help you?"

"Hello," the Technic said, his brown eyes roving over the SEAL. "I'm Lieutenant Mitchell, First Corps, Technic Army. Who might you be?" Neither he nor his fellow Technics wore helmets.

"Bomba," Blade fibbed, thinking of a series of books he's enjoyed in his younger years.

"Strange name," Lieutenant Mitchell commented, still studying the transport. "Where are you from? I have the weirdest feeling that I should know you, and there's something vaguely familiar about your van."

"I'm from Shangri-la."

"Never heard of it."

"But I've heard of the Technics," Blade said. "I didn't know I'd strayed into your territory. I thought the Technics are based down dear Chicago."

"We are. But we call Chicago Technic City."

"I think I like the old name better."

"Did I ask you, mister?" Mitchell responded, his brow knit in contemplation.

"Sorry. I didn't mean to offend you," Blade stated, continuing to beam good-naturedly.

"What are you doing here?" Lieutenant Mitchell inquired arrogantly.

"Excuse me, but I don't see why I should answer your questions when I'm not even in your territory."

"You'll answer them or else," the officer informed the giant. "You're in the vicinity of a top-secret Technic installation, and I'm required to verify the intentions of everyone in this sector."

Blade glanced at the two Technics seated in the rear of the

jeep. Both held Dakon II's. "Really? There's a Technic installation hereabouts? Where is it? What kind of installation is it?"

"Our facility is located in Green Bay, and you would be smart
to avoid the city at all costs," Lieutenant Mitchell said.

"What are you doing there?" Blade probed.

"Do you really expect me to reveal classified information?"

"No, I guess not," Blade responded. "But maybe you can
tell me one thing."

"Which is?"

"I came across several bodies near a wagon earlier. The
people had been torn apart. Do you happen to know what killed
them?"

"We saw them too," Mitchell mentioned. "And no, I don't
know how they died."

"A horrible way to go."

"I agree," Mitchell stated, sounding sincere. He straightened and tried to peer past the Warrior. "Are you all alone?"

"Yep."

"It's dangerous to travel in the Outlands alone."

"I know."

"Have you seen anyone else in this area?"

"No," Blade said. "I'd stopped to eat some jerky when I
saw you driving down the road. Why?"

"You haven't seen anyone at all?" Mitchell inquired.

"Not a soul."

Lieutenant Mitchell exchanged glances with the driver, then
smiled at the giant. "Would you mind if we searched your
vehicle?"

Blade pretended to be shocked by the request. "What?"

"I can't permit you to proceed until I've checked your vehicle.
We're looking for a fugitive."

"And you believe this fugitive might be in my van?"

"There's always the possibility."

"I'm the only one in here."

"I need to be certain," Mitchell said.

"Are you calling me a liar?" Blade asked.

"Of course not. It's just my job."

"Because I am," Blade stated.

"What?"

Blade leaned toward them and lowered his voice in a conspiratorial whisper. "I am, you see."

Lieutenant Mitchell missed the connection. "You're what?" he snapped.

"A liar."

The officer rested his left hand on his Dakon II. "Oh? What did you lie about?"

"Everything."

"Do tell."

"Even my name. It isn't Bomba."

Mitchell shifted, studying the giant's features, mystified by the admission and uncertain of where the conversation might be leading. "What is your real name?"

Blade grinned. "I'll give you a clue."

"I don't want a damn clue. I want your name."

"Where were you three years ago?"

"Three years ago? What difference does it make?"

"Humor me," Blade said. "Think back. What were you doing three years ago this month?"

"I was an instructor at our Training Academy, teaching—" Mitchell began, and amazement set in. He scrutinized the transport, stunned, as if he couldn't believe his own eyes. "You!"

"Me," Blade said, and shot him. The .44 Magnum thundered, the bullet boring into Lieutenant Mitchell's forehead and slamming him against the driver. Blade dropped onto his right side, knowing Sampsom would cut loose, and the burping of the Bushmaster proved him to be right. He waited for the firing to stop, all of five seconds, and popped back up.

The Technics had been unable to squeeze off a single round. Samson had crept to the back of the jeep while the officer conversed with Blade, then risen when the Magnum boomed and poured half of his magazine into their backs. They were sprawled in grotesque positions, their uniforms dotted with red holes.

"Nice job," Blade remarked.

"I dislike shooting anyone in the back, but I couldn't ask them to turn around, could I?" Samson replied.

"You did just fine," Blade assured him.

The jeep abruptly moved slowly forward as the driver's limp foot slipped from the brake pedal.

"What do I do?" Samson asked. "I've never driven a vehicle before."

Blade grabbed the door handle, about to vault out and stop the creeping jeep, when he happened to glance in the side mirror and discovered three more Technic vehicles racing toward the SEAL. They were less than 90 yards away. "Get in! Quick!" he commanded.

Samson looked over his left shoulder, then dashed around the front of the van to the passenger side. "Do we stand and fight?" he asked as he climbed inside.

"No," Blade replied. "They might have grenades. We'll make them come after us, then give them a little surprise." He gunned the engine and took off, accelerating rapidly, his eyes on the mirror.

"What about Yama?"

"He'll wait for us if he returns while we're gone. He knows we wouldn't leave without a good reason."

"I'm surprised he isn't back already."

"So am I," Blade admitted. The speedometer indicated 40 miles an hour and climbing.

"They're gaining on us," Samson commented.

"Perfect," Blade said, and smiled grimly. He saw one of the Technics in the lead jeep talking into a radio. The sight angered him. Now the Technics in Green Bay would know the SEAL was in the area. Now the Mad Scientist, or whoever the blazes he was, would be expecting them.

Typical.

Just once, he mentally noted, he'd like for a mission to unfold without a hitch. Something *always* went wrong. Always. Whether he was on a run for the Family or on an assignment for the Freedom Force, the sequence of events never proceeded exactly as he planned. If a mission ever did go smoothly, he might not be able to stand the shook. The thought made him grin.

"Enjoying yourself?" Samson inquired.

"Are you kidding?" Blade responded. "Who wouldn't have fun on one of our missions? We get to travel hundreds, sometimes thousands of miles from the ones we love the most. We go up against every wacko who comes down the pike. And we have to watch our back every minute of every day while we're away." He paused. "Who wouldn't enjoy himself."

"Forget I asked."

Blade transferred the .44 Magnum to his left hand and extended his arm backwards out the open window, pointing the barrel in the general direction of the three jeeps, not really expecting to hit any of the Technics but hoping to slow them down. He squeezed off a shot and the Technic drivers, predictably, reduced speed.

A curve appeared several hundred yards to the east.

"Do you want me to try and nail them?" Samson queried.

"Save your ammo," Blade advised, withdrawing his arm and sliding the Dan Wesson into its holster. He intended to round the curve, brake, and execute a sharp U-turn. When the Technics came into view, he'd cut loose with the 50-caliber machine guns.

The jeeps were still in hot pursuit.

"Why are there so many Technics this far from Green Bay?" Samson wondered aloud. "Why are they concentrating in this area?"

"My guess is· they're searching for someone," Blade speculated.

"So you think that business about looking for a fugitive was legitimate?"

"Yeah. And if we can find this fugitive before the Technics, maybe we can learn a lot more about their activities in Green Bay," Blade said. He kept the pedal pressed to the floor, gauging the distance between the transport and the jeeps, estimate he would have ample time to complete his maneuver.

Several of the Technics opened fire and a few rounds whined off the rear of the SEAL.

Blade gripped the steering wheel tightly as he neared the curve. He swung the van wide, taking the turn at 60. The SEAL slewed sharply and seemed about to veer off the road into the trees, but came through the curve on all four tires. He went to slam his foot on the brake.

"Look out!" Samson bellowed.

Blade spotted her at the instant the Nazarite yelled, an elderly woman attired in a beige dress who stood in the center of the highway not 100 feet from the curve. He tramped on the brake pedal and jerked the wheel to the right, frantically hoping he could miss her. In the brief glimpse he had of the woman, she appeared to be in a daze, walking westward with her arms limp at her sides and her eyes wide. As the SEAL streaked toward her, a veritable juggernaut of doom, he could see her lined features and gray hair. The van hugged the outside of the road, and for a second he believed he would shoot past her.

And then she did the unexpected.

The elderly woman deliberately stepped into the transport's path.

"Dear Lord!" Samson cried.

Blade wanted to echo his companion, but instead he gaped in sheer horror as the SEAL plowed into the woman, catching her squarely in the middle of the grill. He heard a loud thump, and then the van bounced, as if going over an obstruction. Dreading what he would see, he glanced over his right shoulder.

The woman had fallen onto her left side, and the SEAL's heavy tires had crushed both of her spindly legs to a pulp. Astonishingly, she was trying to push herself up, and her face reflected the same dazed expression. She did not betray the slightest trace of pain.

No screaming.

No hysterics.

Nothing.

"We should help her," Samson said.

Blade slowed, uncertain, bewildered by her demeanor, sensing an alien quality about her. How could anyone be run over by a vehicle weighing tons and not be a bit bent out of shape by the experience?

The Nazarite gazed at the giant. "What's wrong? Why aren't you turning around?"

"Look at her face."

"What?"

"The woman's face," Blade reiterated. He continued to the east at 40 miles an hour, watching in the side mirror.

Moments later the first of the Technic vehicles screeched around the curve. The driver spotted the woman and brought the jeep to an abrupt halt within yards of her still-struggling form. Three other troopers bailed out and hurried to the woman. A lean man, a noncom with four black stripes on his uniform, knelt alongside her. The two other jeeps stopped nearby.

Blade slowed the transport even more, his curiosity getting the better of his prudence. He observed the noncom speaking to the elderly woman, and he was surprised the Technics were so solicitous. His surprise became amazement seconds later when the gray-haired woman reached up and clamped her right hand on the noncom's throat.

"What is she doing?" Samson exclaimed.

The noncom tried to rise. He released his Dakon II and grabbed her wrist. His fellow soldiers came to his aid, attempting to yank her hand free. But she clung to the noncom tenaciously and endeavored to claw out his eyes with her left hand.

"She's trying to kill him," the Nazarite commented, astounded by the development. "Why?"

"I wish I knew," Blade answered absently.

The woman was holding her own, resisting the efforts of the troopers, her fingers locked on the noncom. He beat her on the arm and face, striving to break her choking grip. Another trooper stepped in close and smashed the stock of his Dakon

II on her head. She ignored the blow, concentrating on the noncom.

Blade brought the transport to a halt. He twisted and stuck his head out the window for a better view, confounded by the tableau.

The noncom had risen to a crouching posture, raining punches all the while, swinging his body from side to side, hauling her from the ground. She clung to his neck, her mangled, bloody legs dangling under her, jagged pieces of bone protruding from her pulverizèd skin. Other soldiers pummeled her mercilessly, but she hung on and succeeded in ripping open the noncom's left cheek.

Blade saw a heavyset trooper get out of the second jeep and walk over to the seemingly unequal contest, a pistol clutched in his right hand. The heavyset soldier placed the pistol against the elderly woman's temple and fired. She stiffened, let go of the noncom, and collapsed on the asphalt. Thinking the fight was over, Blade went to turn in his seat when *the woman suddenly sat bolt upright.*

"The Lord preserve us!" Samson breathed.

In complete consternation, Blade watched the heavyset trooper empty the pistol into the woman's head. Only then did she topple over and *stay* down. He exchanged glances with the Nazarite.

"What have we gotten ourselves into?" Samson asked.

"I wish I knew."

Chapter Ten

Yama took two strides toward the stairs.

"Don't!" the brunette wailed, and snatched at his right arm.

The sincerity in her tone and the abject terror she conveyed drew Yama up short. He stared into her petrified eyes, and despite the circumstances of their meeting and the ominous situation in which they were embroiled, he found himself responding to her beauty instead of her fright.

She looked past him and uttered a low groan. "Oh, no!"

Yama faced the stairway.

A man stood framed at the top of the stairs. His clothing consisted of grimy jeans and a faded white T-shirt. Scuffed brown boots covered his feet. His hair and eyes were brown, his hair worn in a crew cut.

"Hello," Yama said.

The man said nothing.

"We're dead!" the brunette declared, backing off. "It's one of them."

"One of the walking dead?"

The man stepped from the shadows with a slow, deliberate tread, revealing a slack countenance and an eerie, vacant aspect to his eyes.

"Don't let him get his hands on you," the brunette warned, retreating toward the stairway to the third floor.

Yama hardly considered the newcomer to be much of a danger. The man possessed the rugged, weathered countenance of a farmer, and although he was slightly over six feet in height and endowed with a muscular build, he came nowhere near matching Yama's superb physique.

The brunette paused at the foot of the stairs and cast a pleading gaze at the man in blue. "Come with me. We can hold them off easier at the top of the stairs."

"I'm not running," Yama said, warily regarding the farmer. "Who are you?" he addressed him. "What do you want?"

No response was forthcoming. The man started forward, raising his arms, and came straight at the Warrior.

Yama trained the Wilkinson on the farmer's stomach. "Don't come any closer," he advised, wondering what the man could hope to accomplish by taking him on unarmed.

The farmer disregarded the warning. Only five feet seperated them. His fingers hooked into rigid claws.

"I won't tell you again," Yama cautioned, surprised when the man completely ignored him.

"Shoot it!" the brunette shouted.

Still exhibiting a blank expression, the farmer took another step and reached for the Wilkinson.

Yama shot him. He squeezed off a short burst, the rounds ripping into the man and flinging the farmer backwards onto the floor. The blasting of the Carbine caused Yama's ears to ring. He walked over to the man and nudged the body, staring at the crimson rivulets flowing from the line of holes across the farmer's midriff.

The man didn't budge.

"Is it dead?" the brunette said anxiously.

"Why do you keep referring to him as an 'it?' " Yama inquired, looking at her.

"Didn't you see its eyes?"

Yama nodded. "He looked as if he was under the influence of drugs."

"Drugs?" she repeated, and snorted at the notion. "If only the reason was that simple."

"What is the reason?"

"I told you. The Mad Scientist has been changing people into the walking dead."

"How?"

"I don't know."

"What proof do you have that the Mad Scientist is responsible?"

"Proof?" she said indignantly. "Who needs proof? Everyone knows the Mad Scientist is behind this. The disapperances didn't start until after that bastard showed up in Green Bay."

"Will you come with me and explain everything to my friends?"

She locked her eyes on his as if attempting to probe the depths of his soul. "All right," she replied after a bit. "I doubt you're a Technic. Maybe I can trust you after all."

"You can. My name, by the way, is Yama."

"Strange name. I'm Melissa," she divulged. "Melissa Vail."

The Warrior smiled and motioned for her to follow him. "Let's go. We must hurry."

Melissa moved toward him. Her gaze strayed to the floor and she suddenly froze.

The short hairs at the nape of Yama's neck prickled as he felt a hand close on his left leg just below the knee. He looked down and an inexplicable ripple of revulsion coursed down his spine as he beheld the farmer slowly rising, using his leg for support. Instinctively, he lashed out, kicking the man in the chest and knocking him onto his hands and knees.

The farmer—or was it truly one of the walking dead?—didn't even blink. He rose and went to clutch the Warrior, his expression as empty as ever.

Yama swung the Wilkinson up and in, driving the barrel underneath the man's chin and snapping his head back. Any ordinary foe would have gagged and fallen to his knees, but not this man. The farmer grabbed the end of the barrel and pulled, displaying tremendous strength, and wrested the weapon free.

"Run!" Melissa urged.

But the Warrior wasn't about to flee. Although he could scarcely believe the Wilkinson had been torn from his grasp,

he was confident his years of experience would enable him to
prevail. Consequently, as the farmer foolishly let the Carbine
drop to the floor, he stepped in close and delivered a palm heel
strike to the farmer's mouth.

The blow rocked the man on his heels. He stayed upright and
took hold of the Warrior's right wrist, striving to draw Yama
into a bear hug.

"If he squeezes you, you're done for!" Melissa yelled.

Yama knew she spoke the truth. His adversary evinced extra-
ordinary might, a superhuman power the equal of three average
men. How such a feat was possible, he didn't know. All he cared
about was defeating the ghoul as quickly as possible, and he
set himself to the task with lethal efficiency.

The man looped his right arm over the Warrior's left shoulder
while continuing to drew Yama's right arm ever nearer.

"Use your guns!" Melissa cried.

Yama had other ideas. He arced his right knee into the man's
groin, but the farmer only grunted. Pressing his left hand against
the thing's chest, he shoved, but the man only moved backwards
an inch. Realizing his foe was on the verge of getting him in
an unbreakable embrace and furious at his failure to escape,
Yama swept his left arm upward, ramming his first two fingers
into the farmer's eyes, gouging his nails deeply.

The ghoul blinked again and again, blood and tears filling
its eyes, and momentarily relented.

Giving Yama the opportunity he wanted. He clamped his right
hand on the farmer's belt, his left on the man's shirt, then slid
his right leg behind the thing and shoved, his steely muscles
uncoiling, employing a standard judo move, a kickback throw,
to toss the ghoul to the floor.

Blinded by the blood in his eyes, the farmer released the
Warrior to wipe his left foreawrm across his face.

And Yama pounced, his right hand held in the Nukite position,
and speared a piercing hand strike at the thing's throat, his
training compelling him to go for one of the softest and most
vulnerable areas on the human body. He felt his fingers sink
into the yielding flesh halfway to his knuckles. Without missing
a beat, as he drew his right hand back, he whipped his left hand

in a Tegatana-naka-uchi, a handsword cross-body chop, connecting on the side of his opponent's neck.

Standing a few feet off, Melissa Vail heard a distinct snap and saw the thing go abruptly limp. "You did it!" she exclaimed in amazement.

The Warrior straightened, his eyes narrowing. "I was lucky."

"You were magnificent," Melissa breathed, her eyes sparkling, her cheeks flushed. "No one has ever broken their hold before. Usually, once one of those things grabs you, it's all over."

"I've never seen anyone behave the way this man did," Yama commented, moving to retrieve the Wilkinson. "It's as if he wasn't responsible for his actions, as if he was a robot."

"Now you know why we call their kind the walking dead."

"We?" Yama said, inspecting the magazine in the Carbine.

"All of us who live in the vicinity of Green Bay. All of my neighbors, my friends, and my family," Melissa said, her voice lowering sadly as she mentioned those dearest to her.

"Did this man live around here?" Yama inquired, gesturing at the slain farmer.

"Probably. He's not familiar to me, but the Technics may have taken him from north or south of the city."

"So the Mad Scientest is taking people from the countryside surrounding Green Bay and transforming them into zombies?" Yama said.

Melissa nodded. "You've finally caught on."

Yama remembered the grisly scene at the wooden wagon and stared at her. "Was your family attempting to get away in a wagon last night?"

"Yes," Melissa answered. "Most of our neighbors had already vanished or been killed, and my dad decided to leave, to abandon this farm instead of staying and being murdered or worse." She sighed wistfully. "Dad figured we could sneak off in the middle of the night when there were fewer Technic patrols. He thought we could outrun the walking dead, but he was wrong. Dozens of them poured out of the forest, blocking the road. Dad tried to turn the team, but the horses were spooked and wouldn't obey him. The next thing I knew, we were being overrun. My older brother fought like a madman and got me into the trees, then went back for Mom and Dad." She stopped, her lips trembling.

"There's no need to go on," Yama told her. "I know what heppened next."

She glanced at him, her green eyes watering. "I wanted to help them, but there was nothing I could do."

"I know."

"They were torn to pieces by those things before I could reach them."

Yama frowned.

"Then they came after me. I fled into the woods, and I was on my way here when you spotted me," Melissa concluded.

"How many of the walking dead have you seen?"

Melissa nodded at the man on the floor. "He was the first since last night."

"We'd better be going," Yama advised. "I must relay this information to my friends." He turned toward the stairs, then stopped in midstride.

Another of the walking dead, a brown-haired woman attired in green pants and a yellow shirt, appeared at the top step.

"I knew there were more in the house," Melissa declared.

Slowly, methodically, the woman came toward the Warrior.

Yama let her have a dozen rounds in the chest and she tumbled down the stairs. He wondered why the walking dead moved so sluggishly. Thank goodness they did! If they should ever acquire the speed to rival their strength, they'd be unbeatable. He took a step.

"Watch out!" Melissa screamed.

The Warrior had already seen the source of her panic, and the unforeseen development dumbfounded him. For there, between the stairway and them, endeavoring to push up from the floor, was the first walking dead, the farmer, who had propped his hands under him and sat up, his head bent at an unnatural angle. Impossible! Yama's mind shrieked. He'd killed the man with his bare hands! Yet the thing was trying to stand. How???

What manner of creatures were these?

What were the Technics *doing* to the people?

All such considerations were removed from his mind an instant later when a portly man stepped into view on the stairs, lumbering toward them. Yama recovered his composure and trained the Wilkinson on the new threat. He'd tolerated all of the delays he was going to, and he resolved to return to Blade and Samson no matter the odds. His features hardening, he fired, sending the portly ghoul flopping from sight. His next rounds drilled into the farmer's cranium and splattered brains and hair all over the walls.

The farmer flattened.

"Stay close to me," Yama instructed Melissa.

"You don't have to tell me twice."

With the brunette almost touching his back, Yama advanced to the top of the stairs and peered down. The black-haired woman and the portly man were gone. But where?

"Be careful," Melissa whispered. "They always travel in packs."

"Can you use a revolver?" Yama asked.

"I can try."

"Here," Yama said, giving her the Smith and Wesson Combat Magnum. "This is a double-action. You can thumb the hammer or squeeze the trigger. Either way the gun will fire."

"Can I club them to death if I run out of bullets?" Melissa quipped.

"Whatever you like," Yama said, and started to descend. Would the things jump them indoors or outside? The creatures would be smarter to attack inside, where the restricted confines would limit Yama's movements. But the walking dead didn't impress him as being exceptionally bright in the strategy department, or any other department for that matter.

A shadow flitted along the wall at the base of the stairs.

What were the devils up to now? Yama inched to the doorway and peeked into the corridor, which turned out to be empty. Hoping the walking dead had opted for easier prey, he hastened toward the front door. The closed front door. Yet he recalled leaving the door open when he'd entered the farmhouse.

"Maybe we should go out the back," Melissa whispered. "They might be expecting us to use the front door."

For the first time since taking off in pursuit of her, Yama

thought of his Near Death Experience and smiled. "Good. I hope they are waiting for us."

"Are you nuts?"

"Whatever these things are, they must be stopped. The more I kill now, the fewer innocent lives will be lost later," Yama stated.

"You can't kill them all."

"I can try."

"You're a hardheaded cuss, you know that?" Melissa remarked softly.

"If you say so," Yama said.

"Don't get me wrong. I like that trait in a man."

"And I like a woman who knows when to keep quiet."

"Is that a subtle hint?" Melissa inquired.

Yama ignored her. He came to the door and opened it without a second thought. The bright sunshine caused him to squint, and he waited a few seconds for his eyes to adjust before striding into the open, surprised to discover no one around. The walking dead, evidently, had departed.

"They're gone," Melissa said. "I don't believe it."

"Do you want me to call them back?"

"Cute. Real cute."

Yama headed in the direction of the highway, retracing his route, but he managed a paltry three yards when the inevitable transpired.

From around both corners of the house, clustered in two groups containing over a dozen men and women each, tramped the walking dead. Silently, balefully, they talked toward the Warrior and the brunette.

Chapter Eleven

"What do you suppose happened to them?"

"Your guess is as good as mine."

"Do you want me to go see?" Samson asked.

"No. I will," Blade said. "You stay here with the SEAL."
He glanced at the Nazarite, who had concealed himself behind
a maple tree a few yards to the east, then left the shelter of the
oak he had squatted next to for the past 15 minutes. What *could*
have happened to the Technics? he mused. Why hadn't they
given chase to the SEAL?

"May the Lord guide your steps," Samson said.

Blade nodded and hurried toward the highway, visible through
the trees 50 yards to the south. To his rear, 20 feet beyond
Samson, camouflaged with limbs and brush and parked in a
clearing where waist-high weeds predominated, rested the
transport. He'd driven the van into the forest to lose the
Technics.

So where were the soldiers?

He'd sped off after the heavyset trooper had shot the elderly
woman, and driven approximately a mile before wheeling into
the woods, expecting the three jeeps would be in prompt pursuit.
But they'd never materialized.

Most strange.

Why would the Technics give up so easily? Normally, the

soldiers would have hounded the SEAL relentlessly. Which convinced Blade that the Technics must have a trick up their collective sleeve.

But what?

He looked in both directions when he reached State Highway 54. The belt of asphalt mocked him with its emptiness. Frustrated, he walked westward, listening for the sound of vehicle engines. His combat boots slapped on the hard surface. A flock of starlings winged overhead. Moments later a bee buzzed past him. He inhaled, savoring the tranquil scene, knowing all too well the respite from the seething violence so prevalent in the postwar era would be fleeting.

It was.

A raspy snarl rent the humid air to his left.

Blade whirled, bringing up the Commando, and spied a slavering mutation standing at the edge of the forest, a two-headed lynx further deformed by a grotesque hump bulging above its front legs. Although nowhere near as big as a mountain lion, a typical lynx was deadly in its own right. And this one wasn't typical. Almost four feet in height and weighing close to 60 pounds, the mutation combined the feral attributes of a wild feline with the deranged thirst for blood of a genetic deviate.

And how Blade despised the deviates!

Ever since his father had been slain by one of the mutated variety, he had hated all mutants with a vengeance. Because of the massive amounts of radiation and chemical-warfare toxins unleashed on the environment during the war, the entire ecological chain had been disrupted, genetically poisoned for generations to come, and the Outlands were infested with the creatures. Everywhere he went, he encountered them. Everywhere he went, he vented his hatred. And like now, he met them head-on, a grim smile plastered on his countenance.

Growling from one mouth and hissing from the other, the lynx crouched and padded forward. A tawny coat of hair covered its body, except for the black tufts at the tip of its pointed ears and the patch of black at the end of its short tail. Its cheek ruffs formed a double beard under its throat.

Blade knew that an ordinary lynx would avoid humans at all

costs. Only the mentally unbalanced creatures, the hideous mutations, characteristically violated the laws of Nature and went after anything and everything they met. He pointed the Commando at the beast's head and was about to fire when the noise of approaching vehicles distracted him.

The vehicles were coming from the east!

From Green Bay!

And suddenly he perceived the tactic the Technics had employed. The soldiers in the jeeps to the west had radioed their base and requested more troops, who were now speeding toward him. The Technics to the west must still be there, waiting patiently to have the SEAL flushed toward them.

Another snarl reminded him of a more immediate danger, and he saw the lynx bounding at him, its lips curled back over its tapered teeth. He cut loose, the rounds boring into the feline's cranium and bringing it crashing down in a disjointed heap. Pivoting, he beheld five jeeps racing toward him, each containing four Technic troopers.

They spotted him at the same instant, and an officer in the lead vehicle began yelling and gesturing.

Blade faced them, fully intending to do battle, but two events transpired almost simultaneously that ruined his plans and put his life in grave jeopardy. First he heard more vehicles approaching, only these were bearing down on him from the west, not the east, and he realized he'd been wrong, realized the soldiers in the three jeeps to the west weren't waiting for the SEAL to be flushed toward them. They'd wisely waited for their reinforcements to reach the area, no doubt keeping in radio contact the entire time, and both forces were executing a classic pincer movement designed to catch the SEAL between them. He glanced to the west and spied the three speeding jeeps.

Even though he was outnumbered, and even though he was caught in the open and wasn't about to plunge into the forest and risk leading the Technics to Samson and the SEAL, Blade raised the Commando and prepared to fire, but a second unexpected development prevented him from squeezing the trigger.

The Warrior heard a bestial growl behind him, and then stumbled forward as a heavy form struck him between the shoulder blades and razor claws sank into his shoulders. In a flash of insight he knew what had attacked him, and he dropped the Commando and reached over his shoulder to grab the animal clinging to his back. Teeth tore into his left wrist, sending excruciating pain along his arm, and held fast.

All the while the thing hissed and snarled.

Blade could feel claws ripping at his leather vest and raking his skin. He whipped his body from side to side, striving to dislodge the brute, to no avail. Next he attempted to flip the beast over his head, but the claws imbedded in his shoulders only dug in deeper. In desperation, knowing the Technics would be on him in seconds, he threw himself backwards onto the asphalt. The animal bore the brunt of the fall. The impact hardly fazed it. With a guttural rumble in its chest, it retracted its claws and scrambled to get free.

Blade rolled to the right and rose into a crouch, drawing both Bowies as he did, feeling his blood trickling down his spine.

Not five feet away, already upright and about to attack, was another vile mutation, the mate of the lynx the Warrior had slain. Like its mate, this one had been born deformed. Instead of two heads, this one had twin humps on its back and an extra leg on each side, undersized limbs that dangled inches above the ground and served no useful purpose.

Blade looked into the feline's blazing orbs and tensed to meet the charge which came a moment later. He slashed both Bowies up and in as the big cat leaped at his head, spearing both blades into the lynx. The creature's momentum bowled Blade over, and he gripped the Bowies and extended his arms, holding the enraged mutation at bay, at arm's length. The strategy worked for a few seconds, until the beast turned its attention to his arms and tore at them with its front claws. He jerked to the right, flinging the lynx from him, letting the Bowies slide out. Both knives were coated with blood, even the hilts, making his hands slippery.

The lynx promptly leaped erect.

Blade pushed to his knees, his eyes always on the cat, and he was ready when the mutation darted at him again. He flicked the right Bowie, going for the beast's eyes, but the nimble cat evaded the knife and circled to the left. Blade turned with it, the Bowies held in front of him. In the back of his mind he worried about the Technics, but he couldn't afford to glance aside or the cat would be on him in a flash.

The lynx silently padded around the giant, seeking an opening.

Blade slowly straightened, wanting to exploit his size advantage, to put more space between his throat and the beast.

Without any warning whatsoever, the mutation sprang, leaping and twisting in midair, going for the Warrior's face.

Blade ducked and buried the Bowies in the mutation's abdomen. His muscles bulged as he sliced the knives higher, cutting into the cat's heaving chest. A torrent of blood spattered his arms and clothes. He swung his arms to the left, hurling the creature to the ground.

The lynx stood slowly. Its internal organs were seeping from the slit. Hissing, the cat glared at the human and coiled for yet another spring.

Blade braced himself. He twisted when the mutation launched itself at him, then drove his right Bowie into the creature's eye. The keen blade went in several inches, splitting the orb.

Unbalanced by the thrust, the lynx alighted unsteadily and nearly fell over. Mustering its flagging strength, the cat righted itself and crouched. Blood and a piece of eyeball were on its left cheek.

Blade decided to end the fight quickly. He feinted with his right Bowie, and when the cat dodged to the left he suddenly lanced his left Bowie into the mutation's left eye, piercing it.

Unable to see, the lynx shook its head vigorously and started to back away.

Raising his right arm, Blade was about to throw the Bowie, to bury the knife in its chest, to finish it off, when someone else took the honor from him.

A single shot rang out and the lynx fell on the spot.

The Warrior spun, his eyes becoming flinty at the sight of the ring of Technic troopers surrounding him. There were five jeeps parked to the east, three to the west, and all of the soldiers from those vehicles now encircled him with their weapons ready to fire.

A black-haired man who wore a different type of silver insignia on his lapels than Mitchell had worn, this time consisting of a pair of thin bars, advanced several feet from the east, an auto pistol clutched in his right hand. He smiled and nodded at the mutation. "My compliments. Few men can take on a mutation with just a pair of knives and live to tell about it."

Blade said nothing. He studied the officer, gauging the Technic as a man who was supremely self-confident and accustomed to a position of authority.

"I trust you don't mind that I killed it for you," the officer said.

The Warrior scanned the soldiers, counting them. There were 32 including the officer. Thirty-two guns were trained on him. The odds were hopeless. If he made a move toward the Commando, they'd turn him into a sieve.

The officer noticed the giant's gaze and grinned. "I trust you're not contemplating any rash act, Blade. I'm under orders to take you alive, but my men will fire if you provoke us."

At the mention of his name the Warrior had glanced at the officer. "You know who I am?"

"There aren't that many seven-foot-tall men running around," the officer quipped. "When Sergeant Nesco radioed in a description of your van, I knew who you were right away. My name is Captain Perinn. I've seen you before. I was stationed at the Central Core in Technic City when Hickok, Geronimo, and you were captured. I saw the SEAL up close."

Blade lowered his arms and sighed. "So what's next?"

"Darmobray wants to see you."

"Who?"

"The Director of our Science Division, the man who heads our Research Facility in Green Bay," Captain Perinn said. "But I'm sure you must know about our Research Facility. Why else would you be here?"

"Would you believe I'm on a vacation and I've always wanted to see Lake Michigan?"

"Not hardly," Perinn replied. "Now if you'd be so kind, place all of your weapons on the ground. And do so slowly. One of my men might become nervous if you make any sudden moves."

Blade had no other choice. He complied, laying the Bowies and the Dan Wesson at his feet.

"Thank you," Captain Perinn said. He walked up to the giant and regarded him carefully. "You have quite a reputation. You know that, don't you?"

"So do the Technics," Blade responded sarcastically.

"You're wasting your breath if you're trying to get me mad," Perinn stated. "And I'm insulted that you would think I'm so immature as to allow a few words to upset me."

"An intelligent Technic. You're a rarity," Blade cracked.

Captain Perinn chuckled. "Always on the offensive, eh? You'd make a great Technic."

"Now who's insulting whom?"

A noncom walked over to them, the same noncom Blade had seen earlier, the one the elderly woman had tried to throttle. He saluted the captain. "Should we return with you, sir?"

"No, Sergeant Nesco," Perinn responded. "Take your men and search for the SEAL. The van must be hidden in the woods nearby."

Nesco nodded, saluted, and began to do an about-face.

"And Sergeant," Perinn added.

"Yes, sir?"

"Stay alert. Blade wouldn't come here alone. There must be other Warriors in the vicinity."

"Will do, sir," Sergeant Nesco pledged, and walked off.

Blade motioned at he noncom. "He's not very popular, is he?"

"Sergeant Nesco?" Perinn said, his forehead creasing. "Why would you say such a thing? All the men respect him."

"I saw a woman try to kill him."

"A woman?" Captain Perinn repeated, then grinned. "Oh. You mean the Automaton. She was a renegade."

"What's an Automaton?"

Perinn holstered his pistol. "I'll leave that for the Director to explain. Darmobray is looking forward to meeting you."

"Why?"

An enigmatic, sinister smile curled the officer's lips upward. "Wouldn't you like to know."

Chapter Twelve

Yama whirled and sent a burst into the group of walking dead who were coming around the southwest corner of the farmhouse. A half-dozen were struck and flung to the ground, but they all immediately began to rise again. He spun to the right and fired at the second group, the bullets smacking into their chests, and dropped five. Like their ghoulish fellows, they promptly stood, seemingly oblivious to the holes in their bodies and their life's blood staining their clothes. Among them were the portly man and the woman Yama had seen inside.

What did it take to kill the things?

"Let's get out of here!" Melissa cried, and raced to the south.

Yama followed, glancing over his left shoulder at the mob of zombielike beings. The beings broke into an awkward jogging gait, and although they weren't very fast, although they could never overtake a normal person on a short haul, Yama entertained the suspicion that the walking dead could run for hours without tiring. A healthy man or woman might outrun them initially, but on a long stretch the superior stamina of the walking dead would ultimately prevail.

"Come on!" Melissa prompted. "Move it!" She sprinted for the trees bordering the south side of the yard.

Reluctantly, Yama followed her. She was bearing to the south instead of the southwest, the direction in which he had to go to rejoin Blade and Samson. He thought about the gunshots he'd heard, and picked up speed.

Melissa attained the woods and paused, waiting for him to reach her, nervously eyeing the walking dead. "Hurry."

"There's no rush," Yama said as he stopped next to her.

"Do you want those things to make mincemeat out of you?"

Yama looked back. The things were a dozen yards off. "We must pace ourselves. Don't wear yourself out or they'll catch you." He angled to the southwest. "Stick close to me."

"Like glue," Melissa promised, running on his right.

They entered the forest and covered 40 yards. The walking dead, impeded by their inability to skirt trees and other obstructions with the same alacrity, fell farther and farther behind.

"Where are we going?" Melissa inquired when they stopped to look back.

"To find my friends."

"Let's hope the walking dead didn't get them."

"No way," Yama said confidently. Blade and Samson would be safe inside the transport. But what if one of them had stepped outside and been surrounded? Troubled by the possibility, he resumed racing toward the highway.

Melissa flew beside him.

They pulled far ahead of the pack of walking dead, and shortly came to State Highway 54. Yama moved to the center of the road and surveyed the highway for as far as he could see. The SEAL was gone.

"Where are your friends?" Melissa asked urgently.

"I don't know."

"Are you sure we're at the right spot?"

Yama nodded, certain they were at the point where he had jumped from the SEAL.

"Maybe they've left you."

"They would never desert me," Yama stated stiffly.

"Then maybe the Technics got them."

The Warrior's features shifted, perceptibly tightening. "We'll head for Green Bay," he announced, and walked eastward.

"We'll *what*?" Melissa asked. She balked at the idea, hesitating, then gazed at the foreboding woods and hastened after him. "Now hold on, handsome. Going to Green Bay isn't a very bright idea."

"My friends and I were on our way to Green Bay. Since they're not here, they must be on their way into the city. Even if they're not, they'll show up there eventually."

"But the Technics have taken over the old University of Wisconsin campus. They control Green Bay."

"I know."

"The walking dead come from there."

"I know."

Melissa blinked a few times in astonishment. "And you still intend to go there?"

"Yes."

"I take back what I said about hardheaded men. You're all a pain in the tush."

The Warrior looked at her. "You don't have to come with me. Hide in the forest until I return."

The proposition seemed to shock her. "You'd leave me here alone?"

"You have the Smith and Wesson. Since you were raised here, you must know this area well. Find a place to hide where the walking dead can't get you. Climb a tree if you have to."

"You'd *really* just up and leave me?"

Yama halted and faced her. "I don't want to leave you. In the short time we've known each other, I've grown rather fond of you."

"You have?" Melissa responded, even more shocked than before.

"If you don't want to go into Green Bay, I can't throw you over my shoulder and cart you there. I'd rather that we stay together, but I'll respect your wishes. If you stay here, it's your decision, not mine."

"How do you mean you're fond of me?"

"I like you," Yama said, and resumed his trek.

Melissa beamed for a moment, then adopted a serious expression and stepped to his side. "You like me how?"

"I think you're attractive."

"You do? In what way?"

The Warrior glanced at her. "Aren't you the least bit

embarrassed talking about yourself?"

"No. Why should I be? I haven't had that many men show an interest in me. I want to know what it is about me you like."

"I can't believe many men haven't been interested in you," Yama remarked. "You're extremely attactive."

"You think so?" Melissa asked, and grinned.

"I know so."

She regarded him critically for several seconds. "I suppose a good-looking guy like you has had a lot of experience with attractive women."

"No."

"Oh? Do you have a girl friend back where you come from?"

"No."

"A wife?"

"No."

"Don't the women there know a good thing when they see it?" Melissa asked bluntly.

Yama grinned, then seemed to stare off into the distance. "There was a woman once, but she wasn't from my Family."

"Were you in love with her?"

"Yes," Yama confessed.

Melissa studied his face, noting a tortured aspect to his eyes. "What happened to her? Did you break up?"

"No," Yama said softly. "She died."

"Disease?"

Yama bowed his head, then cleared his throat and gazed straight ahead. "She was shot."

The agony reflected in his strained tone awakened Melissa to the depth of his inner torment. Finally, here was a man to whom she was strongly attracted, and he obviously had something eating at him. Intense curiosity filled her. "Want to talk about it?"

"Not really," Yama replied, scanning the woods for any sign of the walking dead.

"Sometimes it helps to get things off your chest."

"I've never discussed this with anyone. Alicia's death was too personal."

"Alicia was her name?"

"Alicia Farrow. Lieutenant Alicia Farrow."

"She was an officer? Where? At the place you're from?"

"Alicia was a Technic soldier."

The revelation stunned Melissa. Her eyes narrowed and she gripped his arm. "You were in love with a *Technic*?"

"A Technic who was a woman first, a soldier second. She betrayed her people for me, and she died trying to save my life. Say whatever you want about the Technics, but never insult her."

Melissa released his arm and struggled to compose her swirling emotions. "Were in you Technic City when this happened?"

"No. I'm from a compound located in northwestern Minnesota known as the Home—"

"You're kidding."

"Alicia Farrow and another Technic, a Captain Wargo, came to our Home and made an offer to the Family Elders. They claimed to come in peace. Their leader, the Technic Minister, had allegedly sent them as his emissaries to request our aid in a joint venture that would ultimately benefit all humankind. They said they knew where we could find the Genesis Seeds."

"The what?"

"According to the story they told us, a group of scientists had succeeded in perfecting a new strain of seeds shortly before the war, seeds radically different from those already in existence. There were supposed to be fruit, vegetable, and grain seeds that could grow in barren soil and only needed minimal amounts of water. The Technics said the Genesis Seeds were stored in an underground vault in New York City. They wanted us to venture to New York in the SEAL, that van you saw," Yama related, then sighed. "At least, that was what they claimed."

"And you believed them?"

"The Family had had no previous dealings with the Technics. We were skeptical, but we had no concrete reason to distrust them. They even agreed to leave one of their own people at our compound while the SEAL was away as a pledge of their sincerity."

Insight abruptly flared and Melissa did a double take. "Alicia Farrow?"

"Alicia," Yama confirmed. "We spent a lot of time

together.''

"You fell in love?''

"We grew to love one another, yes.''

"So what happened then?''

"The Technics, you won't be surprised to learn, were lying to us. They wanted to destroy the Family and confiscate the SEAL. They—''

"Wait a second!'' Melissa blurted out, amazement widening her green eyes. "The Home! The Family! Why didn't I make the connection before? You're the ones who took on the Technics and beat them. You're the ones who killed the Technic Minister.''

Yama nodded. "One of the Warriors took care of the Minister.''

"Your Family was the talk of the Outlands.''

"So we've been told.''

"But what happened to Alicia?'' Melissa pressed, feeling guilty about prying but needing to know the details. The Warrior was unlike any man she'd ever known. He radiated a supreme self-assurance and a virile, raw magnetism that attracted her intensely.

"The Technics had a demolition squad lurking outside of the Home, waiting for a signal from her. They planned to sneak over our walls in the middle of the night and set their explosive charges. We found the signal device in one of her pockets, and we assume she sent the signal,'' Yama detailed. "She came up on the rampart and bumped into me. I was on guard duty, filling in for another Warrior, and she was surprised to find me there.''

Melissa remained silent, listening to every word, detecting every nuance.

"She tried to lure me from my post and I became suspicious,'' Yama went on. "At the last minute, when the demolition team was right outside the Home, she had a change of heart and warned me. The Technics scaled our wall. I had hidden on a flight of stairs, intending to jump them when they got closer. Unknown to me, the Technic commandos all had sensitive sound amplifiers in their helmets. They could hear a pin drop at fifty feet. Alicia must have suspected they knew where I was hiding and feared they would mow me down the moment I stood up.''

Melissa scarcely breathed, enthralled by the tale.

When Yama next spoke, his words were barely audible. ''She drew their fire to save my life. One of them cut her to ribbons. I was able to dispose of the demolition squad.'' He paused. ''Alicia died in my arms.''

They covered 20 yards without saying a word.

''There's something I don't understand,'' Melissa mentioned tentatively.

''What?''

''If Alicia loved you so much—and I'm not implying she didn't—then why did she send the signal to the demolition team? How could she want to see your Family harmed, your Home destroyed?''

The Warrior's shoulders slumped. ''She was under the mistaken impression I loved someone else, that I was using her.''

Melissa digested the information for a minute. ''She must have loved you very much to betray the Technics. I've never heard of a Technic soldier disobeying orders before. The Technic bigwigs impose strict discipline on all their people.''

Yama gazed up at the blistering sun and mopped his left hand across his perspiring brow. ''And now they're up to their old tricks again.''

''Actually, they're up to new tricks,'' Melissa said, and grinned.

''Whatever it is, I'm going to put a stop to their scheme,'' Yama vowed.

''Do you want revenge for Alicia's death?''

''I'd like to see them suffer as I have suffered,'' Yama admitted. ''Thanks to the Technics, I experienced the greatest loss a man can know, the loss of the woman he loves. I've harbored resentment of them since Alicia was shot. Maybe if I can repay the Technics in some small measure, I can finally come to terms with her death.'' He glanced at Melissa. ''It's time for me to get on with my life. I can't mope forever.''

''We should live so long,'' Melissa said, staring at the forest on the left side of the highway.

Yama looked in the same direction and saw the line of figures jogging toward them. He recognized the awkward gait instantly.
  The walking dead!

Chapter Thirteen

What should I do, O Lord?

Samson crouched under the sheltering branches of a towering pine tree and watched the Technics load Blade into a jeep. He observed other troopers pile into four other vehicles, and he knew they would depart at any second. The soldiers kept Blade covered at all times. If he tried to rescue his friend, the Technics would probably shoot Blade on the spot. There were simply too many troopers, too many automatic weapons, for Samson to attempt to take them all on alone.

Where was Yama when he needed him?

The five jeeps roared to life. The drivers performed U-turns, and within moments the vehicles were speeding toward Green Bay. Twelve of the soldiers had stayed behind. They were huddled near three parked jeeps, listening to a noncom speak.

Samson couldn't hear the words, but he suspected the squad was about to search the area for the SEAL. He would have done the same if the situation was reversed. Since Blade had told him to stay with the transport, he felt obligated to protect the van. Consequently, he melted back into the vegetation and headed to the north.

If only he could have reached the highway sooner!

He'd heard shots, the familiar thundering of the Commando, and raced toward Highway 54. By the time he'd covered the 50 yards to the road, the Technics had already arrived and were watching Blade battle a deformed Lynx, their Dakon II's trained on the giant.

There had been nothing Samson could do.

He came to a thicket and paused to look back. Sure enough, the 12 troopers were fanning out. Six were walking toward the forest bordering the south side of the highway and the rest were coming to the north, coming toward him.

Samson smiled and eased into the thicket. He lowered himself to the ground and waited. A beetle crawled past his right arm, and somewhere a cricket chirped. While he waited, to compose his mind, he mentally recited one of his favorite Psalms. "Save me, O God, by thy name, and judge me by thy strength. Hear my prayer, O God; give ear to the words of my mouth. For strangers are risen up against me, and oppressors seek after my soul: they have not set God before them. Behold, God is mine helper: the Lord is with them that uphold my soul. He shall reward evil unto mine enemies: cut them off in thy truth. I will freely sacrifice unto thee: I will praise thy name, O Lord; for it is good. For he hath delivered me out of all trouble: and mine eye hath seen his desire upon mine enemies." He smiled, relaxed and ready, and added, "And grant this humble prayer, O Lord. Give me the strength of ten men that your loyal servant might smite those who have transgressed your ordained order."

A pair of soldiers materialized 15 feet off, walking around a tree, their Dakon II's held at waist level. They advanced warily.

Samson watched them intently. He gently placed the Bushmaster Auto Rifle on the ground, then snaked silently to the edge of the thicket. Shielded by the branches and leaves, he put his hands underneath him and coiled his massive arms.

The soldiers came ever nearer, unaware of the proximity of the Warrior, his camouflage clothing rendering him invisible in the thick vegetation.

Samson let them come within a yard of the thicket before making his move. He shoved erect and burst from concealment, stepping between them and looping a brawny arm around each man's neck. His sinews rippling, he swung them almost back-to-back and squeezed.

Both Technics were startled by the abrupt assault. Feeling their breath choked off and unable to employ their assault rifles, they instinctively clutched at the steel bands encircling their throats, endeavoring to break loose. But they might as well have been striving to pry off a boa constrictor.

Samson lifted both men effortlessly into the air, raising their wildly kicking combat boots six inches from the soil. He gritted his teeth and squeezed, squeezed, squeezed. The Technic on the right succumbed first, twitching and sputtering and then going limp. Seconds later the other soldier gasped loudly and stiffened. Samson applied pressure for an additional ten seconds, to be certain, then allowed both men to sprawl on the grass.

Had the other Technics heard the struggle?

The Warrior crouched and listened. Satisfied he hadn't been detected, he retrieved his Auto Rifle and moved stealthily through the trees, seeking other foes. He didn't have far to look.

A lone Technic stood next to an oak tree, yawning, plainly bored by the detail, wishing he was in Technic City instead of a godforsaken forest in the middle of nowhere. Because he considered their search to be a waste of his precious time, he failed to exercise the proper degree of caution. Consequently, he was more than mildly astonished when a pair of iron hands clamped on the sides of his head and twisted sharply. The last sound he heard was the snapping of his own neck.

Samson released the trooper and continued his hunt. He spotted the three other soldiers two dozen yards to the east. They were moving northward, sticking close together, professionals in every respect. He realized he would be unable to catch them unawares, which left him little recourse. Unslinging the Bushmaster Auto Rifle, he sighted on the Technic on the left and fired.

To their credit, the trio displayed superb reflexes. Each man spun toward the Nazarite, and each man received a hail of lead for his effort. They were flung to the earth to convulse and die.

There was no time to lose!

Samson turned and raced toward the highway, anticipating that the remaining six Technics on the south side of the road would hasten to the aid of their companions. He traversed ten yards and came abreast of the wide trunk of a deciduous tree. Stepping to the right, he slid behind the tree and privoted sideways.

Now all he could do was wait some more.

"Where did it come from?" an anxious voice shouted from the vicinity of Highway 54.

"I don't know," another soldier responded.

"This way! This way!" cried a third.

The Nazarite stood stock still, listening to the pounding of 12 combat boots as the troopers drew closer to his hiding place. Their concern for their comrades had made them careless. When he judged them to be within range, he popped into view and cut loose, sweeping the Bushmaster from left to right.

The tactic worked flawlessly.

Only one of the Technics snapped off a few rounds from his Dakon II, and the shots went wild and smacked into the tree next to the Nazarite. The rest all took several rounds in the head or chest and toppled in a ragged line. A tall trooper screamed and thrashed for half a minute before expiring.

Samson ejected his spent magazine and slapped in a fresh one from the pouch he carried on the back of his belt. He ran to the highway, pausing just long enough to ensure all of the Technics were dead. At the edge of Highway 54 he gazed to the east, but the five jeeps were out of sight.

Now what should he do?

His Warrior training dictated his course of action. Whenever a Warrior in the field was separated from his fellows, that Warrior should make every effort to rejoin his companions. The Elder who taught the Warriors had stressed the point repeatedly. His only problem entailed the fact that he was separated from both of his friends. So which one should he go find? Blade or Yama?

The answer became obvious.

Since Blade had definitely been taken by the enemy and Yama might not be in any danger at all, and since Blade, as the head Warrior, was less expendable than Yama, and since the Technics were en route to their facility in Green Bay where Blade might be tortured, or worse, Samson had no option.

He must rescue Blade.

So resolved, the Nazarite walked over to the three jeeps. In one of them the keys were still in the ignition. Although he'd never driven a motor vehicle before, he decided to try. He'd witnessed Blade starting the SEAL many times, so he knew how to get the jeep going. And he'd seen Blade use the brake and the accelerator. He sat down behind the steering wheel and deposited the Auto Rifle in the seat next to his.

Only then did he notice the extra pedal on the floor.

Confused, he stared at the pedal, trying to logically deduce its purpose. The pedal on the right must be the accelerator, and the pedal alongside it the brake, but what on earth did the third one do? Feeling nervous, he prayed to the Lord for a calm mind, then turned the key.

The jeep promptly rumbled to life.

So far, so good.

Samson pressed on the accelerator, but nothing happened. He remembered the automatic gearshift in the SEAL and correlated the shifter with the black gearshift to the right of his seat. He gripped the knob at the top of the shift and tried to move it, producing a series of metallic growling and grinding noises but no movement. Perplexed, he tried the middle pedal, the one he assumed to be the brake, and again nothing happened.

This was getting him nowhere.

He depressed the third pedal and jiggled the black gearshift, and to his relief the shift actually moved toward the dash and seemed to lock into position. Had he done it? He let up on the third pedal and tramped on the gas, and for a fleeting second he felt a surge of satisfaction as the jeep jerked into motion. Unfortunately, his satisfaction changed to vexation almost instantly because the jeep went into motion *backwards*.

Samson slammed on the brake and the jeep stopped abruptly, coughed and lurched, and died. When he attempted to restart it, the vehicle would jump and bounce like a bucking horse. Stymied, he sat pondering his dilemma.

If he took off for Green Bay on foot it would take him hours to get there. Who knows what the Technics would do to Blade in that time? If he could figure out how to drive the jeep, he could reach Green Bay in less than an hour. So whatever time he spent endeavoring to master the vehicle would be well spent if he could get it going.

A big if.

Samson pressed on the third pedal and tried once more. The jeep's motor roared. He fiddled with the gearshift, sliding the stick from the front to the back. When he tried the accelerator, the jeep barely crept along. He eased his left foot off the third pedal, applied pressure on the gas pedal, and the jeep started forward. Delighted, he floored the accelerator, but the vehicle wouldn't go over ten miles an hour. The engine appeared to be straining at the limits of its mechanical endurance.

What could he be doing wrong?

The Nazarite spent 15 minutes trying every combination of pedals and gearshift he could think of, and he'd just about decided to give up and jog to Green Bay when a deep voice spoke to his rear.

"What did that jeep ever do to you?"

Grinning, Samson twisted to find Yama and a brunette standing 15 feet away. Both were sweating profusely and were winded, and the woman had doubled over and was gulping in air as if every breath was her last. "Where have you been?"

"We've been running for the last mile or so," Yama said, coming around to the driver's side. "The walking dead are after us."

"The what?"

"I'll explain later. Where's Blade?" Yama asked, and glanced at the forest.

"The Technics grabbed him," Samson stated.

"And the SEAL?"

The Nazarite nodded to the north. "Concealed in the trees. But it won't do us any good because Blade has the keys."

"Then we'll use this jeep."

"I've been trying to do just that. It might be broken."

"The way you were grinding those gears, I'm not surprised," Yama said. "Remind me to give you driving lessons after we return to the Home."

"You've driven a jeep before?"

"Don't you remember the time I drove from the Home to the Cheyenne Citadel to infiltrate the Doktor's Biological Center?"

"That's right," Samson declared happily, profoundly relieved the chore was out of his hands. "Then you can do the honors and I'll sit back and relax."

"Uhhh, fellas," the brunette interjected.

Both Warriors looked at her.

"I hate to spoil your reunion, but we have company," she informed them, and pointed at the figures approaching from the west, still 200 yards distant.

"Who are they?" Samson inquired.

"The walking dead," Yama answered. "Slide over and let me take the wheel."

"With pleasure," the Nazarite said, complying.

"Hey, what about me?" the woman demanded, hurrying to the vehicle.

"I don't believe we've been properly introduced. My name is Samson," the Nazarite told her.

"Jeez. You're as big as Yama. What do they feed you guys at this Home of yours? Giant pills?"

"If you want to see a giant, you should see Blade, the head Warrior," Samson mentioned. "I didn't catch your name."

"Melissa Vail. I'm going with you."

"You are?"

"She is," Yama stated, sitting in the driver's seat and aligning the Wilkinson between his legs. "Let's take off. Climb in the back."

"Yes, sir," Melissa said. She wearily clambered into the back seat.

Samson leaned closer to the man in blue and grinned. "Have you two known each other very long?"

Yama displayed surprise at the question. "About an hour. Why?"

"You seem to have her well trained. Perhaps the two of you should consider marriage."

"Marriage!" Melissa blurted. "Whoa, there, big guy. Let's not get ahead of ourselves. I hardly know the man." She paused. "And for your information, he doesn't have me trained at all. I'm my own woman, not some pet to be pampered and led by a leash."

"Any woman who married me would be treated as an equal

partner in all of our decisions,'' Yama said, and cranked the jeep over.

"Really?" Melissa responded, leaning forward. "That's nice to know."

Samson glanced from the stony Yama to the admiring woman, and chuckled. "I just hope I'm invited to the binding," he said under his breath.

Yama shifted smoothly and the jeep headed for Green Bay.

Chapter Fourteen

Green Bay turned out to be no different from countless other postwar cities and towns Blade had seen in his travels.

Most of the structures were in varied stages of disrepair. Over a century of neglect and abuse by the elements had resulted in collapsed roofs, buckled walls, and missing or cracked windows. There were exceptions, homes and business establishments maintained in passable condition, but even these appeared to have been recently deserted. Dust and dirt caked everything. Rats scurried in the alleys. Pigeons and other birds flew overhead or perched on poles. A crucial element to any city, however, was missing.

"Where are the people?" Blade asked.

Captain Perinn, sitting in the front passenger seat, glanced back at the Warrior, who sat with an armed Technic on either side, their Dakon II's pressed against the giant's ribs. "Most of the populace are housed at our Research Facility. The others left for a healthier climate." He snickered at a private joke.

"You provide housing at your facility?"

"In a manner of speaking."

"Why are you in Green Bay?" Blade inquired.

"Ask the Director."

"I intend to," Blade promised, wishing he could pound his fist into the smug Technic's face.

"You're about to receive a singular honor," Perinn commented.

"How do you figure?"

"Very few outsiders have been invited into our Research Facility. The Director is treating you as someone special."

"I'm all chocked up."

"We know you Warriors usually travel in threes. You won't be so cocky after we capture your companions," Perinn predicted.

"Never happen."

"Why not?"

"They're smarter than I am. They won't let themselves be caught," Blade said.

"We'll see," Captain Perinn responded.

The jeep convoy had entered Green Bay on State Highway 54, which they had followed all the way to Monroe Avenue. On Monroe they'd driven northeastward to University Avenue, and from there they'd taken Danz Avenue to the East Shore Drive. Now, as they rolled along the south shore of Green Bay, they could see the blue-green water and gulls wheeling in the air.

"Our Facility," Perinn announced, and pointed.

Blade shifted his gaze from the bay to the ten-foot-high barbed-wire fence completely surrounding the University of Wisconsin at Green Bay campus. Two-man Technic patrols walked at regular intervals along the inside of the fence. The lawns beyond had been neatly trimmed, and the buildings repaired and painted where needed. A gate at the southwest corner afforded access to the campus.

"We put a lot of work into refurbishing the university," Perinn mentioned.

"Planning to stay a long time, are you?"

The officer glanced at the Warrior. "Don't you ever give up?"

"No."

"One of these days you'll push too hard, buster."

The vehicles slowed as they neared the gate, where four soldiers stood with Dakon II's at the ready. One of them saluted the lead jeep and Perinn returned the gesture. In moments the gate swung inward and the convoy entered the Research Facility.

Blade glanced at a sign on the barbed-wire fence as they passed within: WARNING! TECHNIC RESEARCH FACILITY A-1 IS OFF LIMITS TO NONAUTHORIZED PERSONNEL. ANYONE CLOSE ENOUGH TO READ THIS ORDER WILL BE SHOT ON SIGHT.

Captain Perinn stretched as the jeeps angled toward a stately building on the south side of the campus. He checked his uniform to ensure his buttons were properly fastened and his insignia were on correctly.

What was the officer doing? Blade wondered. Preening? Or did Perinn's grooming indicate the officer was afraid of what would happen if the Director noticed a dress-code violation? He stared at the three-story building and counted six guards standing outside the entrance.

"A word of advice," Perinn said.

"What?"

"If you should meet my superior officer, don't speak unless spoken to."

"I'll speak when I damn well feel like it."

The officer snorted. "Suit yourself, asshole. But don't say I didn't warn you."

All six guards snapped to attention when the five jeeps pulled up near the stately structure.

"At ease," Captain Perinn stated as he slid to the ground. He smoothed his shirt and waited for the Warrior to be ushered from the vehicle.

Blade glanced at his weapons, lying on the seat next to the driver, and contemplated making a grab for the Commando. But the pressure of two Dakon barrels rammed against his chest stopped him.

"Bring him," Perinn said to the two soldiers, and led the way into the building.

Expecting to find a laboratory, Blade felt a twinge of surprise at the luxurious accommodations he found inside. Plush blue carpet covered the floor. The walls and ceiling had recently been painted mauve, and the walls were adorned with handsomely framed paintings. A wide corridor led to a pair of closed mahogany doors in front of which were four more guards.

"This Director of yours must be paranoid," Blade quipped.

"Don't let him hear you say that," Perinn warned. He nodded at the guards. "I believe the Director is expecting us."

"Yes, sir," responded a youthful Technic. "Colonel Hufford is with him. They said to admit you as soon as you arrived."

Blade noticed the captain tense slightly at the mention of the colonel. Interesting. So it wasn't the Director, after all.

The guards opened the mahogany doors and stepped aside. "Come in, Captain," boomed a deep voice.

Perinn led his party into the inner sanctum, a spacious chamber elegantly furnished with polished furniture, with bookcases lining the walls, and distinguished by a huge desk situated in the very center. Next to the desk, his arms crossed over his stocky chest, stood a scowling officer, gold insignia on his collar.

Blade barely glanced at the glowering Technic. He found the person seated behind the desk to be much more intriguing.

Even though seated, the man at the desk conveyed an impression of immense size. A mane of white hair framed leonine features. His green eyes returned the Warrior's scrutiny fearlessly. He wore a one-piece silvery uniform devoid of insignia or emblems. "Greetings," he declared in his deep voice. "My name is Quinton Darmobray."

"I take it you know who I am," Blade said.

The stocky officer snickered. "So this is the famous Warrior. He doesn't look so tough to me."

"Appearances can be deceiving, Colonel," Darmobray stated coldly. "For instance, someone gazing upon your countenance might mistakenly assume intelligence existed in your cranium."

Blade grinned when the man who must be Hufford straightened and studiously avoided looking at Darmobray.

The white-haired man looked at the Warrior. "To answer your question, yes, I know who you are, and I have been anticipating this meeting with keen relish."

"I didn't realize I was so popular."

Colonel Hufford lowered his arms and took a step toward the giant. "You'll keep your trap shut unless told to talk."

"Or what?" Blade asked. "Are you going to throw a temper tantrum?"

Hufford raised his right fist, as if about to strike the Warrior in the face.

"That will be enough," Darmobray stated coldly. "Colonel, you will leave us alone."

"Sir?" Hufford responded, turning, scarcely concealed anger etching his features.

"You heard me, Colonel," Darmobray said. "I desire to be alone with our guest."

"He's a prisoner, not a guest," Hufford declared. "And since security is my responsibility, I insist on keeping guards with him at all times."

A strange smile creased Darmobray's mouth, strange because it radiated a sinister, chilling intensity instead of warmth and friendliness. "True, security is your responsibility, my dear colonel. But this entire operation is *my* responsibility. I'm the Director of the Science Division, in case you have forgotten, and a close friend of the Minister's. Do you really want me to inform him that you are failing to carry out my instructions?"

Colonel Hufford gulped and shook his head. "No, sir. If you want time alone with the geek, it's yours. But I'll post more men outside your doors and guards outside the windows. He won't escape. I assure you."

"And your personal assurance will undoubtedly aid me in sleeping better at night," Darmobray said with a straight face. "But you need not worry yourself over Blade escaping."

"Why not?"

The Director glanced at he Warrior. "Would you care to enlighten the good colonel or should I?"

"Be my guest," Blade said.

Darmobray riveted his hypnotic eyes on the senior officer. "Our guest has traveled hundreds of miles to reach Green Bay. Unless I'm mistaken, his sole reason for coming was to ascertain the purpose behind our presence in this fair city. He's not about to try and escape until his curiosity has been satisfied. Post your guards, if you must, but refrain from worrying until I *say* you should worry."

"Yes, sir," Hufford responded sheepishly. He motioned with his right arm and all of the troopers filed from the chamber.

Captain Perinn glanced back once and nodded at the Warrior.

Once the double doors were closed, Darmobray rested his elbows on the desk and said, "The captain seems to have developed a respect for you."

Blade said nothing.

"What attribute do you possess that makes men look up to you?" Darmobray asked.

"I'm seven feet tall."

The Director chuckled. "And I am six feet seven. But men only obey me beause they fear me or fear my influence in high places."

"Like with the Minister? I thought we took care of him."

"Hickok disposed of our previous Minister. Naturally, a new one was promptly selected."

"Did the people vote him into office?" Blade inquired.

"Don't be juvenile. The masses are sheep who must be led for their own good. No, our new Minister was duly selected by the directors of the various divisions, of which I am one."

"And probably one of the most prominent," Blade speculated.

Darmobray smiled. "Thank you for the compliment. Yes, you are correct. Next to the Minister himself, I'm the most powerful Technic alive."

"How do your shoulders stand the strain?"

"You misjudge me."

"I do?"

"Absolutely. When I say I'm the second most powerful man in Technic City, I'm not bragging. I am simply stating a fact. My presence in Green Bay demonstrates my influence."

"How so?" Blade questioned.

"Who else could have persuaded the Minister to establish a Research Facility so far from Technic City? Who else would have been granted freedom to do as they saw fit? Who else could have accomplished all that I have accomplished?"

"What exactly have you accomplished?"

Darmobray waved at a chair in front of his desk. "Have a seat, please."

The Warrior sat down and waited.

"What have you heard about our activities here?" Darmobray queried after a bit.

"We were alerted to a series of disappearances."

"Might I ask how you found out?"

"A little birdie told us."

"Fair enough. I wouldn't tell if I were you. But you really have no idea about our true purpose for being here, do you?"

"Not a clue," Blade confessed.

The Director sat back and chuckled. "How ironic."

"What is?"

"That the ancient adage should prove so correct."

"Which adage?" Blade asked.

"Have you heard the one about curiosity killing the cat?"

"I have no intention of dying," Blade stated.

"Please, let's not be morbid. We have so much to discuss before nine tonight."

"What happens at nine?"

"I'll save that for a surprise," Darmobray said. "In the meantime, I'll provide the reason for our being in Green Bray, and later I'll take you on a private tour."

Blade's eyes narrowed. "Why are you being so kind?"

"Because Captain Perinn is not the only one who respects you. Men of our caliber rarely encounter peers of an equal stature. When we do, we should treat one another with the respect we deserve. You and I are not simple-minded idiots." He paused and folded his hands on the desk. "At this very moment, Warrior, you are undisputably the most famous man on the North American continent."

"Give me a break."

"I'm serious," Darmobray stressed sincerely. "Your widespread travels, your encounters with most of the major players on the world stage today, and your adventures in the Outlands have all conspired to make you the favorite topic of conversation around many a hearth and campfire. We know about you, the Russians know about you, you've had dealings with the Leather Knights, the Androxians, and many others. You've probably traveled more extensively across the continent than anyone else. Why should you express surprise at being famous?"

"I didn't come here to hear about my past escapades."

"I know you didn't. You are understandably eager to learn the reason for my activities in Green Bay."

"So what are you Technics up to this time?" Blade inquired.

Quinton Darmobray grinned, his eyes sparkling, and placed his big hands on the desk. "You'll appreciate our purpose, I'm sure. We—more precisely, I—have discovered a technique that, in a few short years, will enable us to rule the world."

Chapter Fifteen

"What's your next move?" Melissa asked.

"We'll sit tight until nightfall, then enter the city," Yama proposed, his hands resting lightly on the steering wheel.

They were on the western outskirts of Green Bay, the jeep parked in an alley between high buildings, hidden in the shadows. Their ride into the city had been uneventful. Neither the Technics nor the walking dead had put in an appearance.

"Is it wise to stay here while Blade is in their custody, my brother?" Samson queried. "Every minute we delay could mean the difference between life and death for him."

"There are too many Technics patrolling the streets for us to venture out now," Yama said. "Under cover of darkness, we should be able to penetrate their security easily."

"Maybe so," Melissa interjected, "but waiting for nightfall is a dumb idea."

Yama glanced over his right shoulder. "Oh?"

"There are more of the walking dead abroad at night. They used to only come out after dark, but that changed a couple of weeks ago and some of them started hunting in the daytime too. If you wait until after the sun sets, the city will be crawling with them," Melissa detailed.

"Where do these walking dead come from?" Samson wanted to know.

"That's easy. The Technic Research Facility."

"Which is where they have undoubtedly taken Blade," Samson said. "I vote we head there right now and try to get inside before nightfall."

"I agree with him," Melissa said.

"Do you think you're coming with us?" Yama asked her.

"I *know* I'm coming with you."

"This isn't your fight," Yama told her.

"The hell it isn't!" Melissa declared. "Those bastards are responsible for the deaths of my parents and my brother. I owe them. I want in."

Yama looked her in the eyes. "This promises to be extremely dangerous."

"So?"

"I might not be able to protect you."

Melissa wagged the Smith and Wesson. "I'll look out for myself, thank you."

"I'd prefer for you to remain with the jeep."

"No way. You're not leaving me alone."

Yama frowned and drummed his fingers on the top of the steering wheel. He gazed at the Nazarite. "Tell her this is no job for amateurs."

"She appears to be determined to go along," Samson observed. "And it has been my experience that trying to change a woman's mind is like beating your head against a brick wall."

"Men don't have any room to talk," Melissa interjected.

Yama reached out and touched Samson's shoulder. "I don't want anything to happen to her."

"You don't?" Samson responded, pretending to be shocked by the news.

"You don't?" Melissa said, sounding delighted.

"No, I don't," Yama reiterated, and regarded her tenderly. "You were raised on a farm, Melissa. You've spent your entire life tending livestock and growing crops. You've never killed anyone and you don't know the first thing about surviving in combat. If you go with us, you'll be committing suicide."

"I'm going, and that's final."

Yama took hold of the keys in the ignition, then hesitated.

"We'd better get our butts in gear," Melissa urged. "The

Technics won't be playing patty-cake with your friend."

"She has a point," Samson noted.

The man in blue started the jeep and slowly drove to the mouth of the alley. After scanning the street, he pulled out and headed northward. "You'll need to direct us to the University of Wisconsin," he said to Melissa.

"No problem. Just keep your peepers peeled for the damn Technics."

Samson checked his Auto Rifle and Bushmaster Auto Pistols, ensuring each weapon was fully loaded. He stared to the west, estimating they had an hour of daylight remaining. Not much time.

"Mind if I ask you guys something?" Melissa queried.

"Anything," Yama replied.

"What are the chances of your taking me back to live at he Home?"

Yama looked at her.

"I'm serious," Melissa stated. "There's nothing left for me around here. My family is dead."

"What about friends and relatives?"

She shrugged. "I have a few, but not any I'm really close enough to that I'd consider living with them. And a woman by herself in these parts is fair game for every wacko who comes down the pike."

"The Elders must approve every application submitted by persons who would like to live at our Home," Yama informed her. "The final decision will be up to them."

"Do you think they'd accept me?"

"You possess talents that would benefit the Family. We can always use another Tiller," Yama said.

"I believe the Elders will accept you," Samson added. "If Yama sponsors you, they will give the application special attention. And I'll second his sponsorship, if necessary."

Melissa studied the Nazarite's rugged features. "Why would you do that for me? You hardly know me."

"I know Yama."

Creases appeared on her brow. "I don't understand."

"As well you shouldn't," Samson said, and let it go at that.

Yama kept to the side streets and alleys as he drove ever

further into Green Bay. Adhering to Melissa's directions, he
bore on a northeasterly course, drawing closer to the bay. As
they were about to take a left from a narrow alley, Melissa
pointed to the right and cried, "Look!"

Both Warriors saw a jeep approaching from the east, filled
with soldiers, perhaps ten blocks distant.

Yama quickly shifted into reverse and backed from view.

"Do you think they saw us?" Melissa asked anxiously.

"We'll soon know," Samson said.

They waited in a tense silence for over a minute, but the jeep
never appeared.

"Stay here," Yama advised them, and hopped to the ground.
He dashed to the mouth of the alley and peeked out to discover
the street clear. The Technics must have turned off on another
street, he realized, and he returned to the jeep.

"Are they gone?" Melissa queried.

"They're gone," Yama verified. He drove from the alley,
hung a left, and resumed their cautious but steady progress
toward the Research Facility. A succession of turns brought
them to a former city park, a three-acre area overgrown with
weeds and brush, located to the south of the site where Melissa
claimed the university would be. He angled into the heart of
the vegetation and killed the motor. "From here on out we go
on foot."

Samson slid down and stretched, his camouflage covered arms
resembling stout tree limbs. "I pray the Lord will grant us
victory."

"I'm beginning to believe there isn't any God," Melissa said
as she jumped from the jeep.

"Why would you say such a thing?"

"Where was God when my parents and brother were being
torn apart by those monsters? How could a loving Deity allow
such atrocities to happen?"

Samson extended both arms, his hands clenched. "Pick a
hand."

"What?"

"Pick a hand," Samson directed.

Hesitantly, uncertain of the Warrior's intention, Melissa
walked over and tapped his right fist. "This one."

"Now you know," Samson said, and smiled.

Melissa glanced at Yama. "Did I miss something here?"

"Now you know how a loving Deity could allow such atrocities to happen," Samson elaborated. "Now you know why God has taken the blame for the evil humanity has perpetuated on this planet. Now you know why God is always made the scapegoat."

"Uh-huh. Would you mind explaining whatever it is I supposedly know?" Melissa asked.

"You just exercised your free will when you picked one of my hands, the same free will every man and woman uses every minute of every day. We use that free will to live a life according to the guidance of the inner spirit or we use it to foster evil. Whoever is behind the walking dead used free will to create a legion of evil. You can't blame Our Lord."

"Excuse me," Yama interrupted. "Could we save the rest of the theology class for later? Right now we have a mission to accomplish."

"All of a sudden he's in a hurry," Melissa said to the Nazarite.

"He's not much for philosphical discussions," Samson responded, grinning.

Yama cradled the Wilkinson and trekked to the north, moving soundlessly, a scowl plastered on his countenance.

Samson leaned closer to Melissa and whispered, "Don't worry. He'll feel a lot better after he's eliminated a few Technics."

"He told me about Alicia."

Samson did a double take. "He did? Already?"

"What do you mean?"

"Nothing. We'd better take off before he has a conniption," Samson advised, and pointed to where Yama stood a dozen yards away impatiently stamping his left foot.

"Is he always this grumpy?"

"Only when his life is in complete turmoil."

The two Warriors and the farmer's daughter advanced through the brush for over a hundred yards before they saw the barbed-wire fence and the buildings of the University of Wisconsin campus. Technic soldiers were everywhere in evidence: at the gate, patrolling the fence, and walking to and from various structures.

Yama crouched in the shelter of a hillock, studying the layout and planning their assault on the Technic stronghold.

"We have about thirty minutes of daylight left," Samson whispered as he came up on the right.

"We're pushing it too close," Melissa commented, kneeling on the left. "The walking dead will be out in force soon. I'm surprised we haven't seen some by now."

"Count your blessings," the Nazarite said.

"We won't be able to scale that fence without being detected," Yama stated.

"How will we get onto the campus?" Melissa inquired.

"We'll go under the fence. Find a couple of thick, broken limbs or sticks we can use."

"Me?"

"Why not you? You're the one who can look out for herself, remember?"

Melissa frowned but obeyed, slipping off to the west.

The moment the brunette was out of sight, Yama turned to his friend. "Promise me something."

"Anything for you, brother."

"No matter what happens once we're in there, no matter what it takes, you'll protect her at all costs."

"Never fear. I know what to do."

"It's strange. I hardly know her, and yet I'm extremely attracted to her."

"You're kidding!"

Yama's eyes narrowed slightly. "For someone who is about to confront superior odds in a fight to the death, you're in a very good mood."

"A healthy sense of humor preserves the sanity."

"Can I quote you?"

"Anytime, brother."

"Just remember what I said about Melissa."

"What did you say?" the lady in question asked, coming around a bush on their left, several sticks in her arms.

"That was fast," Yama commented.

"What did you say about me?" Melissa probed, refusing to let him divert her from the topic.

"That you ask too many questions and never know when to be quiet."

Melissa glared and dropped the sticks at his feet. "Here. You know where you can shove these."

"Feisty wench, isn't she?" Samson commented appreciatively.

"Don't call me a wench."

"Sorry. I meant no insult."

An uncomfortable silence descended for all of ten seconds, at which point Yama scooped up the sticks and moved to the top of the hillock, where he flattened and scrutinized the campus again.

"I didn't mean to snap at him," Melisssa whispered to the Nazarite.

"He understands, I'm sure."

"Really?"

"Well, no, but I thought I'd try and cheer you up."

They crept to the crest and joined the man in blue. The Technic soldiers were still going about their daily routine, and a change of guard was taking place at the gate. Four new troopers were relieving those who had been on duty.

"It must be time for a shift change," Samson said softly. "This could be the opening we need."

Pairs of soldiers appeared to replace those patrolling the barbed-wire fence. Idle conversations were started, and none of the Technics were paying the slightest attention to the outer perimeter. Believing they had the population cowed, and after months without a disturbance, they had grown careless and smug.

"Follow me," Yama directed. He crawled toward the fence, using every bit of available cover, skirting bushes and thickets. In five minutes he came to a clump of weeks and paused to take his bearings. He parted the weeds and received two swift shocks.

Not ten feet away, between the park and the campus, was a wide road.

And approaching from the east, shuffling in a compact mass, their eyes empty and their arms limp at their sides, were hundreds of the walking dead.

Chapter Sixteen

"Once you see my accomplishment with your own eyes, you won't be so skeptical," Quinton Darmobray stated proudly.

"I wouldn't count on it," Blade responded.

They were following a cement walk toward a long, low building situated in the center of the campus. The sun hung above the western horizon and a cool breeze blew in off Green Bay. Trailing behind them came an armed escort consisting of six Technic troopers.

"I should think that you, of all people, should have learned by now not to underestimate our technological accomplishments," the Director commented. "You've seen Technic City. You know what we're capable of."

"You're accomplished marvels with science and technology," Blade admitted, "but you've lost sight of fundamental spiritual values in the process."

"Spiritual?" Darmobray repeated, and uttered a snorting noise. "Oh, yes. I must remind myself that the Family still clings to outdated concepts of truth, goodness, and spirituality. Your people even believe in a supreme Spirit Being, don't they?"

Blade nodded.

"Fascinating. Perhaps, after we have subjugated the Home, I'll prepare a dissertation on the superstitious beliefs of your primitive band of do-gooders," Darmobray said sarcastically.

The Warrior glanced at the Director, who stood six and a half feet in height and weighed a muscularly proportioned 250 pounds at least. "You should live so long."

"Is that a threat?"

"A prediction. Any society that denies the reality of the Spirit is doomed to extinction."

Darmobray snickered. "Is that another sophist tidbit taught by your vaunted Elders?"

"It's the truth."

"Of course it is. And there's a jolly old fat man who lives at the North Pole with his wife, eight reindeer, and one hundred and ten elves."

"What?"

"Santa Claus."

"Who?"

The Director almost broke his stride. "Your Family doesn't believe in Santa Claus, that demented fart who travels around the world in a sleigh once a year scattering reindeer droppings all over the place and delivering shabby gifts to selfish brats?"

"Oh. Him. We read about him during out schooling years, but our Founder didn't perpetuate the practice," Blade disclosed.

"And what about the Easter Bunny?"

"Rabbits don't lay eggs."

"Maybe there's hope for your Family, after all," Darmobray joked. He stared at the structure ahead, his visage sobering. "The Technics don't believe in any of that garbage either. Ever since the war we've discarded all such juvenile notions."

Blade took advantage of the opportunity to glean more information on the Technics' background. "The Technic society first came into being right after World War Three, right?"

"Wrong. *During* the war. A few dozen scientists at the Chicago Institute of Advanced Technology refused to evacuate when the U.S. government gave the order. They held on, using their superior knowledge to forge a new type of society out of the shambles of the old. Instead of exalting the profit motive as the fundamental drive of existence, they exalted the glories of logic and technology. New laws were formulated, designed to promote their philosophy. Those people remaining in Chicago were encouraged to step into line with the new order of things.''

"Encouraged? You mean they became Technics or they died.''

"If they were too stupid to see the light, then they deserved to die,'' the Director stated.

"How convenient.''

"I wouldn't expect you to understand our motives and policies. They're as alien to you as the planet Mars, but they have produced a city and a culture that surpasses any known on earth.''

"Oh, I don't know,'' Blade said. "I've seen a few in my travels that would rival Technic City.''

"I don't believe it.''

"Why am I not surprised?'' Blade asked.

"Our factories and homes are futuristic in the extreme. Our machines and appliances are all computerized and miniaturized. Our people enjoy a standard of living that is the envy of the Russians and the Civilized Zone.''

"Your people are industrial drones who can't escape because Technic City is ringed with mines, wire, and machine guns.''

Darmobray grinned. "Our elaborate security precautions prevent scavengers and mutations from infiltrating our fair city.''

"You can joke all you want to, but sooner or later the millions of people who have had their minds and souls enslaved by the Technic system will rise up in rebellion. There's an old adage. What goes around, comes around. Eventually, the populace you have oppressed will turn on their masters,'' Blade forecasted.

The Director unexpectedly halted and scrutinized the Warrior's features. "So you heard, eh?''

"Heard what?''

"Don't play innocent with me.''

"I haven't the slightest idea what you're talking about,'' Blade said.

Darmobray appeared surprised. "Then you really don't know about the Resistance Movement?''

Insight dawned and Blade smiled. "Another ten years or so and the Technic society will be history.''

"Actually, our computer projections indicate seventeen-point-two years, to be precise.''

"What else did you expect? Your system has taken basic human drives and warped them out of all perspective," Blade remarked.

"Give me an example?"

Blade thought back to his previous experiences in Technic City, to the one revelation that had disturbed him the most. "How about your surrogate parenting program?"

"You know about that?"

"All about the perverted system you've established. Technics believe that the government knows what's best for children, not the parents, so all children are taken from their natural parents at birth and dispensed to surrogate parents to be raised according to the dictates of the Technic doctrine," Blade said.

"Biological bounding inhibits the effective functioning of our devoted citizens. They can't be totally devoted to our Technic order if they're devotion is vitiated by loyalty to their natural parents."

"So the children are yanked from the arms of their parents and given to strangers. They begin compulsory day-care at the age of six months. By twelve years of age they're holding down full-time jobs," Blade related. "The system is disgusting. You deprive your children of the joy of being children."

"An interesting perspective, but I doubt it fully explains the problems which have arisen," Darmobray stated. "A few malcontents have started to stir up the more gullible, ignorant strata of our society against the rulers, against the Technic system itself."

Blade smirked. "And in seventeen-point-two years those malcontents will bring your system tumbling down."

"So our computers assert," the Director said solemnly. "But there is another old adage I'm rather fond of. To be forewarned is to be forearmed. Now that we know the lid is about to be blown off the kettle, so to speak, we can take the necessary steps to ensure the kettle never explodes."

The implications of those words bothered Blade. He glanced at the building they were approaching and felt apprehension gnaw at his nerves. "Is that why you're here in Green Bay?"

Darmobray chuckled. "Excellent. Your powers of deduction rival my own."

"But why come to Green Bay to do whatever you're doing? There are excellent scientific facilities in Technic City."

"The best. Unfortunately, given the nature of the top-secret project in which I'm involved, the Minister and I were afraid there might be a leak. If our citizenry were to learn of my operation, they might rebel en masse before I can complete my studies and implement our plan," Darmobray said.

"So you came here to avoid a security leak?"

"Partly. Green Bay is far enough away from Technic City that I can do my work in private, and it's close enough for the supplies I require to be sent on a moment's notice. This university once included several outstanding labs, and it was a simple task for us to move in and renovate the buildings."

"What is this plan you mentioned?" Blade asked.

"A project so unique, so expansive in scope, and potentially rewarding that we have poured millions of dollars into this operation. My research has received the highest priority from the Minister."

"Which tells me nothing."

The Director grinned and nodded at a green door they were only several yards from reaching. "Why tell you when I can show you?"

"Why bother showing me when you know I'm your inveterate enemy?"

"I'll save that as my final surprise," Darmobray said smugly. He opened the door and motioned for the Warrior to precede him. "After you."

Blade strode into a brightly illuminated corridor. Incandescent lights were suspended overhead. Both the walls and the ceiling had been painted white, and the floor consisted of white tiles. There were a half-dozen doors along each side.

"This is quite a treat for me," Darmobray mentioned. "The only other person to whom I gave the grand tour was the Minister."

"Lucky me."

The Director ignored the crack. "Follow me," he said, and

moved to the first door on the right, which was closed. "Now try not to let your preconceptions distort your judgment." He nodded at the six soldiers, who were standing mere feet away. "If you permit your emotions to get the better of you, they'll shoot."

"Is that a threat?" Blade inquired, mimicking the Director's earlier tone.

"Yes," Darmobray stated. He turned the knob and stepped within.

Bracing himself—or at least believing he was braced for the worst—Blade entered, then stopped, stunned to his core, his mind reeling at the grisly sight he beheld. "Dear Spirit!" he breathed.

"Now don't start with that religious nonsense," Darmobray said, and smiled. "What do you think of my experiemental subjects?"

"If I had my Bowies, I'd castrate you," Blade responded harshly.

"Then I'm in no danger, because Colonel Hufford took your weapons to his office in the dorm the troopers are using as a barracks."

Blade registered the news for later use, gaping at the hapless men and women strapped onto tables covered with rubber mats or sheets. There were ten unfortunates, arranged in two rows of five apiece. All ten were unconscious and attached to life-support systems. They wore white hospital gowns. And every one had been subjected to the same surgical procedure. The tops of their heads had been shaved and sliced into, then peeled back much like an orange peel from an orange, exposing their brains. Oblong black boxes rested on metal stands alongside each table, and a series of multicolored wires connected to the boxes had been inserted into the brain of each victim.

"This sort of reminds me of high school biology class," Darmobray mentioned.

"You're sick, do yo know that?" Blade snapped.

"This is where my research started. This is where I first began conducting my eleborate tests on the human brain, where Project Automaton was launched."

"Project what?"

"Automaton. The term describes my operation precisely. An automaton is someone who acts in a routine or monotonous manner and lacks active intellect. An automaton is also a machine designed to act under its own power, such as a robot."

Blade's mouth slackened and his skin tingled as he realized the ulterior motive behind Project Automaton. "You're making human robots?"

"Close, but not quite," Darmobray said. He walked to the nearest table and placed his left hand on the chest of the supine woman in the detached manner of someone who had no regard for human life whatsoever. "Allow me to elaborate. You see, once we realized that discontent was spreading among our populace, we decided to nip the rebellion in the bud."

"We?"

"The Minister and the directors of the different divisions. As head of the Science Division, the project was put in my hands. Given our computer projections, we knew we had to act quickly. The more dissatisfaction spreads, the harder it will be to stop. So we'll stop it now."

"How?" Blade inquired, his gaze riveted on the woman's brain.

"We realized that our educational system had failed if we couldn't guarantee our citizens were properly indoctrinated in Technic teachings. But we were bewildered because we knew our system was the best it could possibly be. Why then, we asked ourselves, was our system breeding individuals who were able to resist indoctrination and reject the concept of loyalty to the Technic state?" Darmobray talked in a clinical fashion, as if he were instructing a novice Technic. "We came to the conclusion that the fault didn't rest in our system—the fault lay in our citizens. There would always be those who were incapable of assimilating our indoctrination. There would always be those who naturally inclined towards rebellion."

"So instead of changing your system, you decided to change your populace," Blade deduced.

"Improve them would be more apt," Darmobray said. "I hit on the idea about eight years ago, but I wasn't able to implement my experiments until I came to Green Bay."

"What idea?"

Darmobray glanced at the oblong black box to which the woman had been attached. "Where do I begin?" he asked, and paused. "What do you know about the human brain?"

"It's the center of thought and understanding."

"Crudely put, but adequate. Actually, I was referring to the physiological aspects. As you may know, the brain continually gives off waves of electricity which can be measured by means of an electroencephalogram. By tracing this electrical activity, the lines of communication within the brain itself can be traced. Follow me so far?"

"No problem."

"Okay. To be more specific, these brain waves have a frequency of about three to one hundred per second, and a magnitude of only five or five hundred millionths of a volt."

"And all this relates to your Research Facility?"

"Bear with me. Studies have shown normal brains function within a given range of frequencies and voltage. Once the parameters are exceeded, all kinds of problems can result. Grand mal epilepsy, for instance, is associated with beta waves that attain a voltage of one hundred millionths of a volt," Darmobray detailed. "Other studies have demonstrated that different drugs affect the generation of brain waves differently. If strychnine is put directly on an exposed brain, it will increase the frequency and the voltage. Dilantin can eliminate abnormal waves. Even more important, from my point of view, was research that proved that the frequency of brain waves can be increased or decreased by temperatures."

Blade stared at the woman, wondering who she might be and whether she was aware of the wires inserted in her brain.

"I became fascinated by the correlation between brain waves and human behavior," the Director mentioned. "It occurred to me that controlling the frequency and voltage might be the key to controlling conduct." ˋ

"And if you can control human conduct, you can eliminate the Resistance Movement," Blade interrupted.

"If I can perfect my technique, not only will all of our citizens become models of loyalty, devoted to our Technic doctrines, but they'll also do whatever we want without hesitation. Imagine that. Millions of men and women at the Minister's beck and call. His slightest wish will be their command."

"Not to mention the slighest wishes of the directors of the various divisions," Blade noted facetiously.

"Well, us also," Darmobray admitted.

"If you can accomplish your goal, you'll be the envy of every dictator on the planet."

"Won't we, though?" Darmobray said, smiling.

The Warrior pointed at the nearest oblong box. "Is this the technique you're so proud of? You stick wires into someone's brain?"

"Not quite," Darmobray replied. "These are my research subjects. Let me demonstrate." He moved to the woman's oblong box and flicked a switch, activating the device. A row of meters and dials lit up and the box buzzed loudly. "Now watch what happens when I adjust that dial."

Blade saw the Director turn a green dial, and the next instant the womans' arms flapped uncontrollably. The dial was rotated to another setting and her legs quivered. Another turn, and her eyes unexpectedly opened and stared blankly at the ceiling. "Is she alive?" he inquired.

"Technically, she's a vegetable. If I disconnected the life-support system, she'd die," the Director said. He touched the wires attached to her exposed brain. "By inserting the needles attached to the ends of these wires into specific areas of her brain, then regulating the frequency using the black box, I can control her bodily functions."

"How can a person live with their brain exposed?"

"With the proper equipment, they can be kept alive indefinitely. This one has lasted almost a month."

"And I suppose she volunteered to be your guinea pig?"

Darmobray laughed. "She was a farmer's wife, I believe. Her daughter was brought in at the same time, but the girl only lasted a week, as I recall."

A farmer's wife? A mother and daughter who had been brought to the Research Facility together? "Were their names Sandra and Nadine Wolski?"

"Wolski?" Darmobray said, his brow knitting, gazing at the

Warrior in surprise. "Why yes, I believe they were. How did you know?"

"A lucky guess."

The Director's eyes narrowed. "In any event, the experiments I conducted in this room were the first step in proving my theory on how to control human behavior." He walked to the doorway. "Come with me."

Blade exited the revolting chamber of horrors on Darmobray's heels, bearing to the right. "What was the second step?"

"Implants."

"More needles in the brain?"

"No. By implanting a unique tetrode transister into the brain stem, then using a modified broadcast transmitter to emit the proper signal, I can control the behavior of the recipients."

"I don't follow you."

"Okay. Let me explain in greater detail. We have manufactured hundreds of revolutionary transistors, which are tiny electronic devices, mere wafers constructed of silicon. Through a simple surgical procedure, one of these transistors is implanted in the brain stem. They impair normal brain functioning by impeding the brain's electrical activity, in the process transforming the recipient of the implant into an Automaton. To put it simply, they can't think for themselves."

"But how do you control them? How do you get the Automatons to do what you want?"

"That's where the transmitter enters the picture. The implanted transistors are attuned to the specific frequency emitted by our one-hundred-thousand-watt transmitter. When the implants receive the signal, they activate the brains of the Automatons," Darmobray elaborated. "At least, that's the general idea. Unfortunately, the system hasn't been perfected yet. I haven't achieved total control over the Automatons. Most obey the electronic commands incorporated into the transistors. A few renegades don't."

"What sort of commands?"

"Oh, basis instructions," Darmobray said evasively. "It will be another six months to a year before I can successfully, consistently program the Automatons to the point where they almost resemble normal human beings and can perform even routine everyday tasks.'' He sighed. ''I'm still in the experimental stage, but on a grander scale.''

''I saw one of your Automatons try to kill a trooper,'' Blade mentioned.

The Director frowned and nodded. ''I'm not surprised. Eighty percent of the implant recipients obey the commands, but the other twenty percent seem to experience some sort of short circuit resulting in aberrant, violent behavior.''

''Like the woman I saw.''

''Yes. The renegades will kill anyone and everyone they encounter. And they won't respond to the command to return to the Research Facility. They wander aimlessly, in mindless packs, possibly linked in some manner by a subliminal affinity.''

''What about all the people who have disappeared? Have you turned them into Automatons?'' Blade inquired.

''They were abducted by the Automatons. And the majority have received the implants. Dozens have been used on my experimental tables.''

Blade pondered for a moment. ''There's something I don't quite understand. Can the Automatons function if the transmitter isn't on?''

''They're not supposed to, but the renegades do.''

''Let me see if I've got this straight. You transformed some of the residents of Green Bay into Automatons, then used them to abduct more and more people. But about twenty percent of the Automatons developed malfunctions, becoming deranged killing machines.''

''That's it in a nutshell. The Automatons have been programmed not to harm anyone unless they receive a specific command from me,'' Darmobray said.

''And where's this transmitter of yours located?'' Blade queried.

''On the east side of the campus. We erected the special two-hundred-foot-tall tower next to the transmitter. The effective radius is approximately fifty miles, but we plan to increase the range once our system is perfected.''

''Amazing,'' was the only comment Blade could think of to adequately sum up his reaction to the scheme.

Darmobray grinned. ''I knew you'd be impressed.''

"Do you really intend to insert implants into every citizen of Technic City?"

"Once all the kinks are ironed out, of course. The Minister will pass a law requiring every citizen to visit a hospital so they can receive a shot, an inoculation against a fictitious strain of virulent flu. In reality, the shot will knock them out. While they're unconscious, my staff will insert the implants. We should be able to transform ninety-eight percent of the population into Automatons within a two-month span."

"But the people who haven't been transformed are bound to catch on," Blade noted.

"Not at all, because by then my Automatons will be almost normal in every respect."

Blade stared ahead at a wide door blocking the corridor. "So where are you taking me now? To see where you house your Automatons?"

The Director came to the door and halted, his lips creased by a smirk. "No. The obedient Automatons are housed in several buildings in the vicinity of the transmitter. I have something special planned for you."

"Like what?" Blade asked, disturbed by the man's sardonic tone.

"I'm going to implant a transistor in your brain stem and transform *you* into an Automaton."

Chapter Seventeen

Before Yama could let go of the weeds and conceal himself, several of the walking dead gazed in his direction. He knew they could see him, and he expected them to lumber toward him. Instead, they tramped dutifully to the west, heading for the heart of the city. Puzzled, he remained in view, trying to count the number of empty-eyed zombies.

They just kept coming and coming.

The Warrior slid backwards, bumping into Melissa. She gaped at the horde in consternation, her skin pallid. "Snap out of it," he instructed her in a whisper. "We have work to do."

"What do you have in mind?" Samson inquired.

"Let's find out where the walking dead are coming from," Yama proposed.

"An excellent suggestion."

Together they took hold of Melissa and half-carried, half-dragged her into the denser brush farther from the road. She barely resisted until the vegetation screened the walking dead from view, then she shoved them from her and stood. "I don't need your help, thank you very much."

"You could have fooled us," Yama said. "You were petrified."

"I'm fine now."

"Then stick with us," Yama advised, and hunched over,

jogged to the east. Through the undergrowth he could see a line of walking dead stretching for hundreds of yards. They were sticking to the road, apparently venturing forth on their nightly ghoulish prowls. None of the Technics patrolling the fence were in the least bit concerned about the stalking legion.

Why not?

For several hundred yards the trio bore to the east, crouching even lower once they passed the boundary of the former park. Using every available cover, whether it might be a bush, a tree, the rusted hulk of an automobile, a ditch, or an overgrown hedge, they continued until they came to a junction where another road angled to the north.

At the southeast corner of the fence encircling the university stood a second gate, which hung wide open. Through the gate came the last of the walking dead.

Yama dropped flat 20 yards from the road. The sun had started to dip below the western horizon and ever-lengthening shadows were creeping across the countryside. He gazed at the gate, confused. Why did these walking dead totally ignore the Technics guarding the campus, and yet the woman he had seen earlier had almost killed that noncom? Did the Technics possess a means of controlling the ghouls? If so, what was it?

The four guards posted at the southeast corner swung the metal gate closed and locked it.

Samson crawled to within inches of Yama's right arm. "This is becoming stranger and stranger by the minute."

"What do we do now?" Melissa asked, sliding up to the man in blue from the left.

"The first step is to get inside," Yama said softly.

"Do you have a brainstorm on how we can accomplish that little feat?" Melissa cracked.

Yama gazed at the backs of the walking dead, then at the gate, and smiled. "As a matter of fact, I do," he replied, and began removing his weapons.

"What are you doing?" Melissa asked, perplexed.

"Watch and learn," Yama advised her. He placed the Wilkinson, the Browning, and the scimitar next to Samson. "Don't let anything happen to these."

"I'll guard them with my life," the Nazarite responded, and he meant every word.

"Are you planning to surrender?" Melissa asked sarcastically, and received a shock when the man in blue nodded.

"Yep," Yama said, and crawled closer to the road, his eyes on the Technic quartet at the gate. They had turned and were staring at a small building approximately 50 yards to the north of their post. Only then, when he glanced at the same structure, did he spot the tower. Surprise made him pause. Why hadn't he noticed the thin metal spire earlier?

Two hundred feet in height, the strange spire had been painted to blend into the sky, to be invisible on the skyline. Only six inches wide at the base and less than an inch from the 100-foot mark on up, the tower was an engineering marvel, reminding the Warrior of a sewing needle, an *enormous* sewing needle.

What purpose did it serve? Yama wondered, and stood, allowing his arms to hang limp at his sides. He adopted the blankest expression he could, widening his eyes and letting his mouth droop open, and plodded forward onto the road, making a beeline for the gate.

One of the guards happened to look over his shoulder. The Technic privoted, his forehead furrowing in bewilderment, and blurted, "What the hell is this action?"

His three companions swung around.

"Look at that geek!" the heaviest of the soldiers said, and snickered.

"They are the biggest bunch of morons on the planet," chimed in another.

"This one doesn't have the brains of a shrimp. He's going in the wrong direction."

"They don't have any brains, stupid," declared the first guard. "That's why they're called Automatons."

"Well, what the hell does this one want?"

"Maybe he has to take a leak," the heavyset soldier joked.

Ignoring their taunts, Yama shuffled right up to the gate and halted.

"Get lost, freak!" snapped one of the men.

"Yeah," added heavy butt. "Go the other way, damn your

hide!''

The first guard, who seemed to be in charge of the detail, moved closer to the man in blue. "He can't understand you. The things get their instructions from the Director.''

"Oh yeah? How, Mr. Scientist?'' demanded the heavy trooper.

"I don't know all the details, but the transmitter has something to do with it,'' the leader said, and gestured absently at the building to the north.

Interesting news, Yama thought, his visage a stony, hopelessly stupid, mask.

"Why don't you shoot the jerk, Ted?'' suggested the heavy Technic.

"Oh, sure, Yoder,'' Ted replied. "And have my ass hauled in front of Colonel Hufford? Are you crazy?''

"So what do we do with it?'' Yoder inquired. "Turn it around and give it a boot in the ass?''

"It couldn't hurt,'' said another.

"Whatever we do, we can't harm the thing,'' Ted stated. "You know the orders. No wasting these Automatons unless they've turned renegades.''

Yoder came to the gate and peered at the Warrior. "How do we know this freak hasn't gone over the edge?''

Ted chuckled. "When they blow a fuse, you know it. They go wacko. This one would be clawing at the fence or trying to climb over to get us.''

"Maybe so,'' Yoder said. "But I still don't like them. The Automatons give me the creeps.''

"Hey, Yoder,'' spoke up one of his fellows, "did you ever think that the feeling might be mutual?''

Everyone except Yoder enjoyed a hearty laugh.

"Have your fun, dipshits,'' Yoder snapped. "You'll all get yours one day.''

Ted reached for the lock, produced a key from his fatigue pants, and sighed. "What worries me is the rumor that the Director plans to create more of these things.''

"What the hell for?'' Yoder asked. "Aren't there enough already?''

"I wish I knew. The whole project is hush-hush,'' Ted

remarked. He inserted the key, twisted, and the lock snapped open.

"Tell us about it," muttered the leanest Technic. "How come they won't let us contact our wives? I'd like to write Martha, but we're not permitted to send letters until the Director gives the okay."

"Which could be next year," Yoder said.

"I'll tell you this," Ted mentioned as he pulled the gate inward. "This is the last damn time I volunteer for a special assignment. I know they promised us extra pay if we took this rotten duty, but I had no idea what I was getting myself into. Hell. I've been here since day one and I still don't have any idea."

"Join the club," Yoder declared.

Digesting the information they were inadvertently revealing, Yama stood perfect still. Let them come to him. Under his blue uniform his arms tensed.

Ted motioned for the silver-haired Automaton to enter. "Come on," he beckoned. "This is what you want, right?"

The Warrior didn't budge.

"I still say we should shoot the thing," Yoder cracked.

"Maybe we should let the Director know," suggested the lean trooper.

"I'd rather call Perinn. At least he's decent," Yoder said.

Ted stepped out and grabbed the Automaton's left wrist. He tugged, then tugged again when his first effort had no effect. "Come on. Let's go," he prompted, and yanked hard.

"What's the matter? Can't you handle one of these freaks?" Yoder baited him.

"I'd like to see you do any better."

"Oh, hell. Let's do it, fellas," Yoder proposed, and they converged on the man in blue. Yoder took hold of the thing's right arm, his mouth scrunched up distastefully. "I just hope whatever this geek has got isn't contagious."

"I can safely say that's the least of your worries," Yama told him, assuming his normal poised posture, and in the seconds it took them to react to the startling development, before they could unsling their Dakon II's, he went into action. The tip of his right boot slammed into Ted's crotch, doubling the trooper over, even as he whipped his right arm free of Yoder's grasp and knifed the rigid tips of his fingers into the heavyset soldier's throat.

The remaining two Technics went for their weapons.

Yama leaped into the air, wrenching his left arm loose from Ted in the process, and kicked, lashing out with his right foot. The sole caught one of the troopers on the chin, snapped the man's head back, and sent him stumbling backwards. In midair Yama twirled, driving his left leg down and out, and rammed his foot into the last soldier's chest, knocking the Technic to the pavement.

Ted tried to connect with an undercut aimed at the Warrior's groin.

But Yama twisted, evading the punch, and alighted in the cat stance, coiled to strike. A swordhand chop into Ted's nose flattened the trooper's nostrils and flipped Ted onto his back. A snap kick spiked Yoder under the chin, lifted the heavy man from his feet, and toppled him to the ground.

Still game, the other two were clutching at their Dakon II's.

Yama took a stride and delivered a spin kick to the head of the Technic on the pavement, flattening his foe. The only soldier in any condition to fight had managed to unsling his Dakon and attempted to point the barrel. With a slight hop and a vaulting leap, Yama reached his adversary, his right foot connecting against the trooper's sternum.

A loud snap sounded, the Technic gasped and bent in half, and the last sensation he felt was the calloused edge of the Warrior's right hand arcing into the back of his neck.

In the horse stance now, Yama stood ready to attack or counter, and surveyed the quartet. All four had been rendered temporarily or permanently insensate. Satisfied, he scanned the campus, expecting to hear a cry of alarm. None sounded, and he promptly stooped and began dragging the Technics to the side of the fence.

Footsteps pounded and Samson and Melissa appeared, the Nazarite bearing Yama's arms.

"You were sensational!" Melissa breathed in awe. "How did you do that?"

"Ants in my pants," Yama replied, lugging Yoder from the

gate opening.

"You've got to teach me how to do that," Melissa stated.

"Teach you the martial arts?"

"Is that what it's called? Yeah. Teach me the arts."

Yama almost made the blunder of erupting in laughter. Instead, he toted the lean trooper to one side. "Which one of the . . . arts . . . would you like to learn?"

"There are different ones?"

"All kinds of styles and disciplines."

Melissa shrugged. "I don't know. Teach me the deadliest art."

Yama grabbed Ted and dragged the Technic off. "The deadliest art, huh? That would be the Leonardo."

"Yeah. Sounds great. When we get out of here, show me how to do the Leonardo."

"You've got it," Yama promised, keeping a straight face only with a monumental effort. He noticed that Samson had developed an inordinate interest in the darkening sky.

"So what do we do next?" Melissa asked eagerly.

"*We?*" Yama nodded at the Nazarite, who promptly returned his weapons.

"Well, you know what I mean."

"I would suggest that Samson and you stay here and watch this gate while I go find Blade," Yama recommended.

"Why should we be stuck at the dumb gate?" Melissa inquired.

"Because we will need an avenue of escape once Blade is free. Ensuring the Technics don't block our retreat is critically important," Yama noted.

"Oh. In that case, we'll watch the gate. No one will take it from us," Melissa vowed.

"Tell that to them," Samson interjected, and nodded at the road bordering the south side of the university.

Yama glanced in the indicated direction, and despite his years of experience he felt a knot form in his stomach at the sight of the horde of walking dead who had, incredibly, reversed direction and were coming toward the southeast corner of the fence, toward the very gate through which they had departed and which now hung wide open.

Chapter Eighteen

"If you don't lie down on the table now, I'll have you shot," Quinton Darmobray vowed.

Blade stared at the six Technic troopers, at the six Dakon II barrels pointed at his chest, then at the metal table in front of him. A thin sheet composed of a rubberlike substance covered the top. On the other side of the table, arranged in a neat row on a small stand, were surgical instruments.

"This is the last warning you'll receive," the Director said.

Reluctantly, fully aware the scientist meant every word, Blade complied and reclined on the table. His legs dangled over the bottom edge from his knees down.

Darmobray smiled and stepped alongside the small stand. "That wasn't so hard, was it?"

"Get stuffed."

"I would expect a more mature riposte from a man like you," Darmobray stated. He reached under the edge of the rubber sheet, which hung several inches below the table's rim, and pulled a leather restraint into view, drawing it higher. The other end was obviously attached to the metal table.

Blade blinked twice. "What's that for?"

"Don't be naive. What do you think it's for? I told you a simple surgical procedure is used to insert the transistor, and I need you to lie perfectly still while I'm placing one in your brain stem."

A flinty light seemed to animate Blade's gray eyes as he coldly regarded the restraint. If he allowed his arms and legs to be fastened to the table, he'd be unable to prevent the Director from implanting the device that would transform him into an Automaton. But if he resisted, the six troopers would shoot him.

Or would they?

Blade looked at Darmobray, who stood on the right side of the table, then at the soldiers, who were all standing to the left and within two yards of his dangling legs. An idea occurred to him, a means of possibly thwarting the Director's plans and regaining his freedom.

"Why do you think I went to so much trouble to explain my operation at you?" Darmobray was saying. "You're an exceptional man, an adversary I can respect. I wanted you to fully appreciate the extent of my genius while you were still in possession of your faculties." He paused, smiling expansively. "And imagine what a victory this will be for the Technic order when the mighty Blade is reduced to the status of a mindless slave! The Minister will be delighted. I might even receive the Royal Order of Service, the highest award a Technic can receive, for this."

Absently listening to the Director babble, the Warrior scanned the room, searching for possible weapns. The dimensions were 24 feet by 24 feet, with a ceiling ten feet high. Banks of computers and other electronic equipment lined three of the walls. The fourth, the west wall, contained the wide door. There were three other tables in the room, aligned to the right of the one on which he reclined. His was the nearest to the doorway. The only window occupied the east wall.

"Besides, I want to test my device on someone of your stature," Darmobray went on. "With your exceptional conditioning and steel willpower, you might even be able to resist for a few seconds once you awaken from the operation. I'm very curious to learn whether you will become an obedient Automaton or a renegade. Knowing you, I'd wager the renegade."

"Thanks for the compliment."

The Director grinned maliciously. "Think nothing of it. Now, if you would be so kind as to give me your hand?"

Blade did, but not in the manner which Darmobray expected. Having decided upon a course of action, he galvanized into motion with lightning rapidity. His right hand shot toward the Director and seized the front of the scientist's silvery uniform. In the blinking of an eye he hauled Darmobray onto the table even as he gouged his left hand into the man's throat.

Predictably, the six Technic troopers tried to bring their Dakon II's to bear, but before any of them could snap off a shot the Warrior had interposed a thrashing shield. None of them were about to fire when they might hit the Director.

Blade clamped his left hand on Darmobray's neck and held the gurgling, wildly swinging Technic at arm's length. ''Drop your weapons!'' he commanded, barely feeling the weak punches landing on his head and shoulders. His blow had dazed the Director and made the scientist red in the face, and it would take Darmobray at least a minute to fully recover. Which was all the time he needed.

The soldiers hesitated, perhaps out of fear of the consequences if they relinquished their Dakon II's on their own initiative.

''Do it or I'll snap this bastard's neck!'' Blade snapped, and shook the Director for emphasis. Darmobray sputtered and tried to speak, but the best he could do was squeak.

With a resigned detachment, five of the troopers lowered their assault rifles. The sixth, though, a crafty devil with a sneer on his countenance, opted for fame and a surefire promotion if he could save the Director. He suddenly lunged forward, trying to step past the end of the table for a clear shot at the giant. But in his haste he made a mistake.

Blade merely swept his legs up and out, his combat boots slamming the man in the mouth, and sent the Technic sprawling onto the floor. In the same motion he slid off the table on the right side, his muscles bulging and rippling as he raised Darmobray overhead, all 250 pounds of him. He glimpsed the Technic's startled expressions, then hurled the scientist with all of his might. Without waiting to observe the result, he whirled and dashed to the door.

Behind him arose a tremendous crash and the mingling of curses and exclamations.

His right hand grabbed the knob and twisted, and as he tugged on the door a Dakon II chattered and rounds smacked into the jamb on his right. Another second saw him in the corridor, the door shut tight. He estimated he had all of ten seconds before they were after him, ten seconds in which to elude them. Four strides brought him to a closed door on the left. Aware that every moment could mean the different between life and death, he opened the door and slipped into the inky interior, and not until the door was shutting did he abruptly perceive that he had entered a utility closet. His fingers tightened on the doorknob and he was about to continue his flight when he heard upraised voices.

Darmobray and the troopers!

"—skin you alive if he gets away!" barked the Director.

"What else could we do, sir? He would've killed you."

"I don't want to hear your lame excuses. Fan out! Find him!"

"Where could he have gone?" asked a trooper.

"Am I a mind reader?" Darmobray responded, his voice rising shrilly. "*Find him!*"

Blade tensed as boots tramped in the corridor. He held fast to the doorknob, and it was well he did because someone took hold of the other side and attempted to wrench it open.

"Hey! This door is locked! Maybe he's in here!" called out one of the soldiers.

"That's a closet, you idiot!" the Director snapped. "A man like Blade is not about to allow himself to be trapped in a utility closet. Check all the rooms, all the windows!"

"Yes, sir," the Technic responded.

The pressure on the doorknob eased and Blade relaxed, listening to the troopers pound off in the direction of the entrance. Temporarily, at least, he had a respite, and he used the reprieve to plot his next move. Acquiring weapons was paramount, and the weapons he wanted the most were his Bowies and the Commando. According to Darmobray, they were in Colonel Hufford's office in the dorm the Technics had converted to a barracks. But which bulding would it be? There were so many on campus it would take him an hour to go to every one.

The corridor had gone quiet.

Blade eased the door out a crack and peeked to his left, toward the exit at the far end. None of the troopers or the Director was in sight. Muffled voices came from several of the rooms as they conducted a thorough search. If he attempted to sneak past them, they were bound to spot him. And eventually, Darmobray notwithstanding, they would get around to checking the utility closet.

Where was the one place they would least likely expect him to be?

The operating room.

Blade scanned the corridor again, then slipped from the closet, closed the door, and raced to the operating room, trying to avoid slapping his combat boots on the tile. He intensely disliked turning his back to his enemies, but it couldn't be helped, and now he had done it twice in as many minutes. His shoulder blades tingling, he came to the operating room, ducked within, and shut the door.

Whew!

The Warrior hurried to the window and inspected the sill, finding a latch which he promptly released. He raised the window enough for him to pass through, then leaned out and surveyed the lawn and the nearest structures. The encroaching darkness shrouded the landscape in benighted shadows. There were no troopers in sight, so he slid over the sill and dropped to the ground.

Which way?

Staying in the gloom at the base of the wall, he bore to the right, constantly alert for Technics. When he reached the corner he paused, then cautiously inched his eyes to the edge.

Thirty feet away, their weapons slung over their shoulders, conversing idly, slowly approaching the rear of the building, were two soldiers.

Blade retreated several yards into the blackest shadow and crouched, his brawny hands flat on the ground. He was surprised that the Director hadn't sounded an alarm, and he wondered if the Technics simply hadn't bothered with a security system because of the logistics involved. The huge size of the campus and the number of buildings would have entailed expending a lot of time and resources, and perhaps they had figured the fence and their patrols were sufficient.

The pair of troopers stepped into view at the corner.

Just as a siren cut loose with an ear-splitting whine.

So much for his bright ideas! Blade thought, and sprang from concealment. The Technics had spun and were staring back the way they had come, sitting ducks. He leaped behind them, took hold of each man by the scruff of the neck, and pounded their heads together before either of them knew what was happening. Both sagged, but neither was unconscious, and they tried to reach over their shoulders to grasp his arms. With a powerful sweep of his titanic sinews, he bashed them together once more. The trooper in his left hand slumped, but the one in the right still struggled.

The siren continued to wail.

Impatient to be off, Blade rammed the Technic in his right hand against the buildings, then let them both drop. He appropriated their Dakon II's and ran to the west.

Shouts arose in different directions.

Go! Blade's mind shrieked.

Go!

Go!

Go!

He flew to the front of the building, and as he bounded into the open he glanced to his right and saw his sparring partners from the operating room. His abrupt advent took them unawares, and five of the six merely gaped. The sixth, Old Crafty Face, exhibited astonishing reflexes, bringing his Dakon II up the instant he saw Blade.

But the Warrior was quicker.

Blade fired both Dakon II's simultaneously, his initial rounds boring into crafty puss and flinging the trooper to the grass. He swept the assult rifles back and forth, mowing the five others down, their chests and heads exploding in miniature crimson geysers, and emptied the Dakon II's into them. They died without screaming.

The Warrior dropped the assault rifles and headed to the southwest, in the direction of the gate through which he had entered the university. If he couldn't locate the dorm soon, he intended to at least escape the Technic's clutches.

"Over this way!" yelled a man off to the right.

"What's going on?" demanded another.

Blade heard them clearly, and he suddenly realized the siren had ceased. Thankful for small blessings, he sprinted onward and spied a long two-story structure directly ahead. Through the double doors at the west end came four troopers, two in the act of donning their uniforms.

Was that the barracks?

The Warrior doubled over, minimizing his outline, and hoped they wouldn't see him. They were glancing every which way, clearly perplexed, not knowing where the campus might be under attack. One of them said something and they all moved to the southwest.

How convenient.

Blade grinned and poured on the speed. When he was ten feet from the double doors another Technic emerged, this one buttoning his shirt.

The soldier heard the Warrior and looked up.

"Surprise!" Blade quipped, and delivered a devastating right to the man's nose. The impact hurled the trooper into the doors, his nostrils crushed, his eyelids fluttering. A second right drove him to the ground.

A hasty scrutiny verified no other Technics were in the vicinity, so Blade went through the double doors into an office containing a desk and several chairs. Past the office, extending the length of the building, was a hall lined with a dozen doors on each side. He halted near the desk and looked at a closet in the left-hand corner, the only likely spot where his weapons might be stashed.

Blade darted to the closet and tried the knob, which turned readily, and a moment later he stared happily at the Commando, propped against the right side, and his Bowies and the Dan Wesson on the floor. He stooped to scoop up the knives, and as he did the double doors were flung outward and in came Colonel Hufford and Captain Perinn.

Chapter Nineteen

"Dear God!" Melissa exclaimed in horror. "What do we do now?"

"You shouldn't take the name of the Lord in vain," Samson said.

"More to the point," Yama remarked, "why are the Automatons returning now? The guards weren't expecting them back to soon." He closed and locked the gate.

"Automatons?" Samson repeated quizzically.

"That's what those things are called," Yama disclosed. He stared at the legion of the dead, now 75 yards distant, and remembered the comment the Technic named Ted had made about the transmitter in the building to the north, the structure next to the strange spire. If the transmitter somehow controlled the Automatons, then perhaps the transmitter could be used to stop them.

"Let's get the heck out of here!" Melissa proposed.

Yama glanced at the Nazarite. "Can you hold this gate?"

"Until Hell freezes over."

"Hopefully, I won't be gone quite that long," Yama said. He pointed at the building housing the transmitter. "I have reason to believe I might be able to stop them from there."

"Then go. And may our Lord guide your hand," Samson stated sincerely.

"What about me?" Melissa blurted.

"You can help Samson hold the gate."

"Against all of *them*?"

Samson caught Yama's eye and shook his head just once, so that Melissa wouldn't notice. "I'll hold the gate by myself."

"Are you sure?"

"Go. Time is wasting."

The man in blue glanced at the Automatons, nodded grimly, and jogged to the north. "I won't desert you. I promise."

"I know," Samson responded.

Yama held his Wilkinson at waist height and stayed close to the fence, scrutinizing the small structure. On the south side a solitary window, covered inside by a white shade, cast a diffuse ring of light around its rim.

"What do you want me to do?" Melissa whispered.

"Exactly as you're told."

"You're enjoying this, aren't you?"

The Warrior ignored the question, concentrating on a tree that had materialized approximately 30 feet from the transmitter building. He angled toward it, casting a quick look over his left shoulder.

Only 40 yards separated the Automatons from the gate.

Yama speculated on whether the transmitter operator might have seen him dispatch the guards and had ordered the walking dead to return to slay him. He crouched down as he neared the tree, and was gratified to observe Melissa do the same. The woman learned quickly. She had brains as well as beauty, and a feisty temperament to boot. What more could a man ask for?

What the hell was he doing?

Thinking about her at a time like this!

They came to the tree and knelt on the grass.

Yama gazed back at the gate and the road. The lead row of Automatons was just passing under one of the perimeter lights the Technics had positioned at 40-foot intervals along the fence. They were 30 yards from Samson.

"Look!" Melissa declared softly, and indicated the building.

The Warrior swung around and saw a door on the west side. Someone had left it hanging open about an inch. "Stay here," he directed her, and hastened to the structure. He paused at the corner to survey the campus grounds for troopers, and once satisfied there were none nearby, he eased to the door and stood listening.

"—very dangerous, sir," a man was saying.

"I don't give a damn," snapped a deep voice.

"With all due respect, Director, we've never attempted to work them into a killing frenzy before. Only the renegades have killed. If we drive all of the Automatons over the edge, they may go berserk and slay us as well," stated yet another person.

A five-second silence ensued.

"Now you listen to me, you quislings," the man with the deep voice declared. "You'll do exactly as I say, or I will personally report this to the Minister and persuade him to ship you both to work at a worm farm."

"We have your welfare in mind too, Director," said the first man. "The procedure is extremely dangerous. What's to stop the Automatons from killing you?"

"Are you hard of hearing?" the Director thundered. "I want you to increase the power, and I want you to do it *now!* As the Director of the Science Division, I command you to obey me!"

The Director of the Science Division? Yama peered into the building. There was only one room. Occupying half of it, and situated against the opposite wall, stood a rectangular metal cabinet containing an array of dials, switches, and meters. Two men, both wearing green smocks, were busily manipulating the controls while a third man watched, an imposing white-haired figure attired in a white uniform, his back to the door.

"As soon as you have made the proper adjustments, we will join our soldiers who are grouping at the southwest gate," the white-haired man said, and his voice identified him as the Director. "Colonel Hufford and his men will protect us. We'll abandon the Research Facility until the job is done."

One of the men in green glanced around. "And all this for just one man, sir?"

"Not just any man, Epson. We're talking about the man who has become the greatest threat to the existence of our Technic order since Technic City was founded. One of his colleagues brutally murdered our previous Minister. And he has caused us no end of grief. Well, it all stops here. Now we have him trapped, and I want him dead within the hour."

Yama had tensed at the mention of the previous Minister. Since Hickok had been the Warrior, the Director must be referring to Blade!

"We'll draw the Automatons onto the campus," the Director was saying. "With the transmitter at full power, they'll be impelled into a killing rage. They'll range all over the university, going from room to room, hunting for victims." He paused and cackled. "And the only one left on campus will be Blade!"

Yama had overheard enough. He flung the door inward and stepped inside and to the left so he wouldn't be framed in the doorway, the Wilkinson leveled at the man they called the Director. "Don't touch that transmitter!"

All three men spun to face the Warrior.

"Who the hell are you?" the Director demanded.

"Raise your arms," Yama directed, wagging the Wilkinson. The two technicians complied, but the Director simply glared.

"Who *are* you?"

"I'm the man who is going to put a hole between your eyes if you don't do exactly as I tell you to do," Yama warned, and took a bead on the center of the man's forehead.

Glowering, the white-haired man obeyed. "Do you know who I am?"

"Ask me if I care."

"I'm Quinton Darmobray, fool. The Director of the Technic Science Division. And you, if I'm not mistaken, must be another Warrior."

"Yama."

"Damn! You sons of bitches are crawling out of the woodwork."

"Where's Blade?"

"I haven't the slighest idea," Darmobray said. "Your giant friend escaped a short while ago."

Yama looked past the trio at the transmitter, his gaze roving over the bewildering complexity of the controls. "How do you turn that thing off?"

"Wouldn't you like to know?" the Director retorted.

The Warrior took a half stride forward. "The Automatons are approaching the southeast gate. I want you to stop them."

"And if we don't?" Darmobray sneered.

"I'll kill all three of you."

The Director placed his hands on his hips and thrust his chest out. "Go ahead, smart guy! Kill us! But our deaths won't stop the Automatons from smashing through the gate, and you can't stop them by yourself."

Yama pointed the Wilkinson at the transmitter. "And what's to stop me from simply blowing that thing apart?"

"You do, and you'll have more trouble on your hands than you can imagine. A sensitive transistor has been implanted in the brain stem of each Automaton. If you shoot up the transmitter, you might cause each transistor to short. If that happens, the pain will drive them berserk."

"Isn't that what you wanted?" Yama asked suspiciously.

"Yes, but I wanted their killing frenzy to be conducted under my control. After allotting them enough time to slay Blade, I intended to return and reduce the power output, thereby regaining total domination over my mindless slaves," Darmobray said. "But your way, no one could control them."

Unsettled by the news, and distrustful of the Director, Yama mulled his options. The idea had seemed so simple. Destroy the transmitter and the Automatons would drop in their tracks. But now what should he do? He couldn't risk transforming the creatures into crazed berserkers, not when Samson would be trying to hold them back at the gate.

The thought made him frown.

How was the Nazarite faring?

The advancing legion of the dead were ten feet from the gate when Samson trained the Bushmaster Auto Rifle on the foremost ranks and shouted, "Stop! I don't want to harm you!"

Unheedful of his warning, their expressions devoid of all animation, the Automatons tramped closer and closer.

For an instant Samson's resolve faltered. Melissa had been right. There were so *many*! Row after row after row of zombielike beings who were impervious of injury. He recalled the woman on the road, clawing at that noncom even though her legs had been crushed, and he inadvertently shuddered.

Five of the walking dead came to the gate and took hold of the metal bars.

Grant me strength, O Lord! Samson prayed, and squeezed the trigger, going for the head in each instance, his rounds drilling through craniums and felling the five where they stood. But as soon as they fell, there were five more to take their place. He shot them, and on came more, seven this time, and even as he fired at them a sobering realization sent a chill down his spine.

What would happen when he ran out of ammo?

Samson's lips compressed. He saw the Automatons fan out, going to the right and left of the gate, and several started to climb awkwardly up the barbed-wire fence, oblivious to the sharp barbs gouging their hands and tearing into their bodies. The sight filled him with a peculiar, and totally uncharacteristic, dread. They were like persons without souls! For an awful moment he imagined himself to be battling the soulless legions of the Evil One, alone against the Hordes of Hell.

He fired and fired and fired.

At the first sound of the Bushmaster, Yama tensed, recognizing the distinctive chatter.

The Director also heard the shots. "That's not a Dakon II," he said, and his eyes narrowed. "It must be one of your friends. Is the fool trying to stop the Automatons?"

Yama knew he had to do *something!* If he couldn't wreck the transmitter, then he might be able to locate an off switch. He stepped to the left-hand wall and motioned with the Wilkinson. "Line up against the right wall," he ordered.

Darmobray and the pair of technicians did as they were told, lined up with the Director nearest the doorway. "Have another brainstorm, did we?"

The Warrior sidled to the transmitter and scrutinized the dials and meters. One of them must shut the damn thing down! To his consternation, he discovered that none of the controls were labeled. The Technics were thwarting him at every turn. But then, the bastards always were plotting and scheming and conniving to outwit and subjugate innocent people who only wanted to be left alone to live their lives as they saw fit. Just as Alicia and he had wanted to do.

But no.

The Technics could never leave well enough alone.

They were power mongers determined to impose their beliefs on everyone else, no matter the cost in human suffering.

A cold, simmering fury gripped Yama and he swung toward the trio. They were no longer in front of the transmitter and he didn't have to worry about accidentally hitting the cabinet. "How do you switch the transmitter off?" he asked once more, his tone flat and hard.

The two technicians blanched. Darmobray only snorted.

"Suit yourselves," Yama said, and shot the technician on the left, three quick rounds through the man's green smock high on the chest. The force of the slugs propelled the technician into the wall, and he slumped to the floor trailing crimson streaks on the white paint.

"Having fun?" the Director joked.

Yama turned his attention to the second tech. "How do you switch the transmitter off?"

His eyes widening in abject terror, the second technician trembled and blurted out, "I'll tell you! I'll tell you anything you want to know!"

"You'll do no such thing!" Darmobray barked.

"He'll shoot me!" the tech wailed.

"Don't tell him!" Darmobray hissed.

Yama took a step toward them. "Show me how to turn the transmitter off," he instructed the technician.

"Gladly," the man said, and went to comply.

Yama glanced at the Director, expecting Darmobray to try and stop the tech, and it was well he did. He saw the scientist look at the doorway and perceptibly stiffen, and the Warrior instinctively threw himself backwards and pivoted.

A Technic trooper stood just outside the doorway, a noncom sporting four black stripes on his uniform, a Dakon II held firmly against his right hip. He had already activated the Laser Sighting Mode, and the red beam of light was centered on the Warrior's torso when his trigger finger began to squeeze. He thought he had the man in blue dead to rights, which made him all the more astonished when he missed. The Dakon II, on full automatic, sent 15 of its 30 rounds into the transmitter before he could check is fire.

Yama snapped off a burst, the Wilkinson booming in the small building. His shots were accurate, catching the noncom in the neck and head and knocking the man to the ground. He heard a loud crackling and fizzing and glanced at the transmitter, appalled to see the outer casing fractured and smoke wafting toward the ceiling. Tiny reddish-orange sparks and flames sparkled inside. In the moment he was distracted by the sight, he glimpsed movement out of the corner of his right eye.

Quinton Darmobray was ignominiously fleeing through the doorway.

And the second technician, his features contorted by a look of maniacal desperation, bunched his slim fingers into fists and leaped at the Warrior.

Blade's outstretched fingers were six inches from the Bowies, and the distance might as well have been light years for all the good it did him. Hufford and Perinn, both of whom wore side arms, were already going for their weapons. In a twinkling, he whirled and sprang, executing a flying tackle, his boots leaving the floor, his body arrow straight.

"You—!" Colonel Hufford blurted.

And then the Warrior plowed into them, angling his body between the two Technics, his broad shoulders ramming into their hips, his huge arms encircling their waists. The momentum drove them backwards, into the double doors, and all three crashed down in the doorway with the soldiers bearing the brunt of the impact.

Blade reared to his knees and whipped his right fist in an arc, his knuckles striking Captain Perinn on the chin just as the officer lifted his head, flattening the trooper.

"You bastard!" Colonel Hufford snarled, scrambling from under the giant and shoving to his feet. His right hand clawed for his pistol.

With all the swiftness of a rattler, Blade jabbed a punch into Hufford's abdomen, doubling the man over. He surged up off the floor, his left arm rigid, his palm vertical, and raked the heel across the colonel's face, drawing blood from the mouth and the chin.

Grunting, Hufford staggered rearward, out the partly open doors, still endeavoring to unholster his gun.

Blade went after the Technic, not letting up for an instant. He delivered a right to Hufford's ribs, then a left, and with each blow the stocky colonel gasped and tottered, spittle dribbling from his mouth. Hufford bent in half, wheezing, and Blade snap-kicked the tip of his right boot into the soldier's head.

As if struck by a ball peen hammer, Colonel Hufford catapulted onto his back.

"Nice moves."

The Warrior spun, startled to behold Captain Perinn standing five feet away, a pistol in the Technic's right hand.

"Damn, you're fast!" Perinn said, the words distorted by the blood rimming his mouth and flowing out the right corner. The Warrior's punch had crunched his teeth together, and caused his upper central incisors to tear into his lower lip.

Blade tensed, waiting for a sign that the Technic intended to squeeze the trigger, intending to launch himself at the proper instant.

"The Director buzzed just a few minutes ago," Perinn said, dabbing at his mouth with his left sleeve, and nodded at a portable military field radio resting on the desk. "He told us you'd escaped and ordered the colonel to collect all the man together at the southwest gate. We were on our way there when the colonel remembered he'd left your gear in the closet." Perinn paused and grinned. "He didn't want you to get your hands on your weapons, so we came back."

"What now?" Blade asked, inching forward slightly.

"The Director wants you in a bad way. He's got something special planned for you, but I don't know what it is."

Blade assumed the trooper must be referring to the implantation. He prepared himself for a headlong rush, wishing for a distraction and getting his wish.

Unexpectedly, Colonel Hufford gurgled and started to rise.

Captain Perinn glanced down at his superior officer for a fraction of a second, and perceived even as he did that the giant was in motion, coming right at him. He automatically fired.

The Bushmaster Auto Rifle went empty and Samson tossed it aside. He'd used the last of his spare magazines, and now had to rely on his Auto Pistols. His hands swooped to the swivel holsters strapped around his waist, holsters he had designed himself and the Family Gunsmiths had constructed. He took hold of the synthetic pistol grips and swung the barrels up. Both breakaway holsters parted at the seams, and he immediately snapped off rounds at the walking dead, felling six in rapid succession.

But still they came on. The Automatons had now spread out in a 40-foot line along the fence and were attempting to scale the fence in their slow, methodical fashion.

So far Samson had been able to hold his own and keep the ghouls out. They were ridiculously easy targets as they came to the top of the fence or the gate, and he picked them off one after the other. The dead littered the ground. For a brief moment he believed he had overreacted, that the Automatons weren't that much of a threat.

And then it happened.

All of the walking dead inexplicably stiffened, their entire bodies going rigid, their eyes wide as saucers. For seconds they stood perfectly still. Suddenly, incredibly, they began to jerk and twitch and flail their arms, walking in small circles, their heads rocking from side to side. Those on the fence fell off.

Dear Lord! Samson marveled. What was happening? He lowered the Auto Pistols, confounded. What could have caused them to act so bizarrely?

The grotesque dance of the dead persisted for a full minute, and ended as abruptly as it started. Reeling or swaying, the Automatons stood in place, their facial features locked in outlandish grimaces.

What now? Samson wondered.

And the very next second he received his answer when the creatures, as one, turned toward the campus and renewed their assault on the security fence. Only this time their attack was different, this time they went about their task with a vengeance, striving to pull the fence down and batter through the gate, their countenances reflecting a feral madness, an unquenchable bloodlust. Despite the wounds they had sustained, they ripped and tore at the barbed wire, their blood spraying the ground.

The Nazarite opened up with the Auto Pistols, slaying foes as swiftly as before, but now they were moving faster and making more progress, and even though he killed and killed, they succeeded in breaching the fence, in tearing down a six-foot section to the left of the gate.

The instant the fence crumpled, the Automatons poured through the gap.

They were inside!

Samson retreated a few yards, firing as he did, emptying the left Auto Pistol and then the right. Before he could hope to reload, they swarmed upon him. He was forced to discard the Bushmasters and resort to his malletlike fists, slugging every Automaton that came within reach of his steely sinews. Every blow produced a resounding thud and sent an Automaton to the ground. He swung to one side, then the other, to the rear and the front, always in motion, a human whirlwind endowed with the power of a dynamo.

But even dynamos have limits.

Because Yama had tried to bring the Wilkinson to bear on the fleeing form of the Director, he was unable to compensate and train the barrel on the second tech before the man reached him.

The technician uttered a piercing scream, perhaps to spur his flagging courage, and swept both of his fists at the Warrior's exposed throat.

Yama deftly blocked the man's arms, using his left forearm to batter the technician aside, then smacked the barrel across the man's temple, staggering his foe. He brought his right knee up into the tech's crotch, and the man screeched at the top of his lungs. Using the Wilkinson stock, Yama clubbed him twice.

His eyes rolling upward in their sockets, the technician collapsed.

An acrid odor filled Yama's nostrils, and he rotated to find the transmitter in flames and bright ribbons of electricity arching between several of the internal components. He remembered the words of the Director: "If you shoot up the transmitter, you might cause each transistor to short. If that happens, the pain will drive them berserk."

Samson!

Yama spun and raced from the building. He sprinted toward the tree, wondering what could have happened to Melissa and why she hadn't warned him about the noncom. When he reached the tree, he understood. The sight he beheld transfixed him and stirred him to the depths of his soul.

The walking dead had breached the fence and were swarming around Samson in a frenzied effort to bring the Nazarite down. They punched and clawed and tore at his camouflage fatigues, a crazed pack of rabid jackals striving to slay a mighty lion. But Samson was proving to be the equal of his namesake. He rained a torrent of blows on the Automatons, his fists steely pistons, his bony knuckles thudding into foe after foe after foe. Dozens upon dozens were already down, the majority never to rise again, their foreheads caved in or the skulls split open. Yet still they came on, and it was clear the Nazarite was beginning to tire.

A scream tore from Yama, a scream that originated in his gut and tore from his throat unbidden, a scream of commingled rage and affection for one of his few, true friends, a scream the likes of which he hadn't voiced in more years than he could remember. *"Samson!"*

Yama ran toward the battle, realizing he couldn't use the Wilkinson because he might accidentally wing the Nazarite. He took ten strikes, and only then did he spot Melissa, not 15 feet in front of him. She was on her knee, holding the Smith and Wesson with both hands, apparently ready to fire. "Melissa! Don't!" he shouted.

She glanced around as he sped to her side.

"You could hit Samson," Yama told her before she uttered a syllable.

"But—" Melissa began.

"Here. Take this," Yama ordered, and shoved the Wilkinson at her.

"What? Why do—"

"Take it!" Yama snapped.

Startled, she grabbed the weapon. "What are you going to do?"

"Stay here. If the Automatons come after you, head for the west side of the campus. You might be able to sneak out without being spotted by the Technics."

"But what about you?" Melissa asked, too late, because the man in blue had dashed off and was now rushing toward the southeast gate. She glanced at the machine gun in her left hand, perplexed. How was he going to fight the walking dead without it?

Her answer came a few moments later.

With her heart pounding in her chest and her blood pulsing in her temples, Melissa Vail saw the silver-haired Warrior whip his scimitar from its scabbard and, without breaking stride, hurtle into the midst of the walking dead. The flashing blade gleamed in the glow from the perimeter lights, and in the space of six seconds, a half-dozen Automatons were sent to the turf with their necks nearly severed or their faces split asunder.

The scimitar seemed to be in perpetual motion as Yama ripped into the horde of ghouls, spinning from one side to the other, always spinning, his keen blade biting deep and drawing blood with every stroke. His unexpected onslaught temporarily stemmed the inhuman tide, and he actually succeeded in fighting his way to Samson's side. The Automatons checked their attack, disoriented.

"What kept you, brother?" the Nazarite quipped, panting from his exertion, a grin twisting his lips.

"I was darning my socks," Yama quipped, and took up a position behind his friend, his back almost touching Samson's.

"Seen Blade?"

"Nope."

"Figures. Maybe Hickok is right after all."

"About what?"

"About us doing all the work and Blade goofing off all the time."

And then there was no more time for words. The Automatons renewed their bestial, mindless assault, pressing in from all sides, reaching for the two Warriors, their sheer force of numbers creating a living ring of impending death around the man in blue and the Nazarite.

To Melissa, watching the unequal conflict in impotent despair, the outcome could never be in any doubt. Yama and Samson were felling the walking dead in droves, but for every two they killed there were four more to take the place of the dead ones. Sooner or later, the Warriors would be overwhelmed. She rose, intending to aid them in whatever way she could.

That was when she spied the four Automatons coming for her!

Blade saw the Technic's finger tighten on the trigger and he twisted a millisecond before the pistol discharged. He felt a stinging sensation in his right side, and then he had his hands on Perinn's neck and his right knee drove up and in, sinking into the captain's ribs. There came a loud snap, and the officer gasped and doubled over, the pistol pointing at the ground.

Colonel Hufford had collapsed again.

With his right thumb extended and rigid, Blade swept his right hand in a tight loop. He buried the thumb all the way to the knuckle in Captain Perinn's throat.

The Technic's eyes bulged and he clutched at his neck.

Aware that more soldiers might arrive at any moment and thwart his escape attempt, Blade grabbed both sides of Perinn's head and wrenched his arms in a vicious twist.

Another snap sounded, louder this time, and Captain Perinn slumped and sprawled onto his stomach.

Blade never bothered to examine his handiwork. He hurried inside and over to the closet, and within a minute had the Bowies in their sheaths, the Dan Wesson in its shoulder holster, a..d the Commando in his hands.

Now let the Technics try to stop him!

He stepped from the building and moved to the right. Off to the southwest, visible between two trees and illuminated by perimeter lights, was the gate through which he had entered the campus. Amazed, he watched a convoy of Technics preparing to depart. Evidently, every trooper assigned to the Research Facility was leaving.

But why?

Blade surveyed the university, studying the stately structures and the surrounding grass. No more Technics were in evidence. Thoroughly puzzled, he happened to glance to the southeast.

What was that?

He took several paces, his eyes narrowing as he tried to make sense of the bewildering jumble of swirling people. They were too far off for him to identify any faces. It looked as if a general melee was in progress. Were the Technics involved? He listened for gunshots, but there were none.

What in the world?

Blade advanced farther, and his eyes detected the glimmering flicker of a long, bladed weapon, a sword perhaps, or a—scimitar! He darted forward, his legs flying, a feeling of foreboding arising and lending speed to his limbs.

Dear Spirit!

Let him be in time!

He covered the ground with a speed belying his size. The scene he observed when he finally came close enough to distinguish details confirmed his worst fears. The pair of stalwarts in the middle of the conflict were unmistakable.

Samson and Yama were laying about them with all the lethal expertise at their command. Automaton bodies lay in piles. Some of the zombies were convulsing and thrashing, waving the stump of an arm or trying to secure their head in place when they had been almost decapitated.

Blade was about to toss the Commando aside and join the fight when motion off to his left drew his attention to a solitary woman who was about to take on four Automatons. She was fumbling with a weapon, Yama's Wilkinson, and if she didn't fire soon they would have her. "Get down!" he bellowed.

She looked up, saw him, and instantly flattened.

The giant aimed carefully and squeezed off a burst, aiming high, going for the heads of the Automatons. His rounds smacked into them from an angle slightly behind and to the left, propelling them forward onto their knees or flat on their chests. One of them almost hit the woman.

Blade placed the Commando at his feet, drew both Bowies,

and sprinted toward his fellow Warriors. The automatons were concentrating on their intended victims, and none of them realized a new menace had arrived until he flew into them, the Bowies slicing right and left, impaling them from the rear or the side, taking them any way they came, never still for a second, always slashing, slashing, slashing. He towered over them, a veritable colossus, his rippling muscles splattered with their blood and gore.

Samson saw the head Warrior first. His arms and shoulders ached from his continual barrage of blows, and his reflexes were slowing. "Hear your servant, O Lord!" he prayed. "Grant me the strength of twenty!" With the thought came a surge of power to his limbs, and he fought on, crushing Automaton after Automaton to the earth. He spun to the left, and a thrill ran through him at the sight of Blade, not ten feet away, pressing toward them, cutting like a madman with his prized Bowies. Samson let out a whoop and flattened an adversary.

Yama heard the yell, and in the back of his mind he was astounded that the Nazarite would vent a cry of delight when they were being pressed upon on all sides by the walking dead. He arced the scimitar into the neck of a burly Automaton, then pivoted to slice his blade into the head of a deranged woman. As he tugged the scimitar loose, he found himself facing to the west.

And there was Blade.

"Back to back!" the giant shouted, and fought to their side in an awesome display of primal savagery.

"Glad you could make it," Yama yelled.

Blade, Samson, and Yama formed into a triangle, their wide shoulders within two feet of one another, leaving just enough space for the giant and the man in blue to wield their blades effectively and for the Nazarite to employ his fists. They took on all comers, rooted in place, refusing to be budged despite the dozens who charged each of them. The Bowies, the scimitar, and those malletlike fists downed Automatons with staggering rapidity. The corpses formed into heaps around the triumvirate of death and destruction, and the walking dead who tried to clamber over their slain comrades found themselves at a fatal disadvantage. All the Warriors needed was the slightest opening and their enemies were doomed.

Stupefied by the sight, Melissa Vail knelt on the cool grass and witnessed a tableau the likes of which few mortals had ever laid eyes on. She saw the trio slay Automatons by the score, saw them stab and thrust and punch until they were covered with crimson and bits of flesh and hair, saw them kill and kill until there were no more Automatons left to slay, until the Warriors stood triumphant on the field of battle, upright amidst a sea of vanquished zombies. Only then did she speak, an innocent, inadvertent comment that summed up all she had been through since encountering Yama, and at the same time a poignant question concerning her future.

"Dear God! What have I gotten myself into?"

Chapter Twenty

The Warriors had found enough explosives stored in a locked building on the north side of the campus to destroy the Technic Research Facility, and before departing Green Bay they set off a blast that rocked every structure in the city.

Melissa sat in the back of a jeep being driven by Blade, next to Yama. She gazed at each of the men, reflecting on her decision to travel to the Home.

"It will be a long time before the Technics try a stunt like that again," Blade predicted.

"I hope so," Samson said from his position in the front passenger seat. He stretched and stared at the road ahead.

"It's unfortunate that the Director and the rest of those soldiers got away," Yama mentioned.

"We'll cross swords with Darmobray again," Blade stated. "He's not the type to take this loss lying down."

"I can't wait," Yama responded.

"There's one thing I don't understand," Blade commented.

"What's that?" Yama asked.

"Why did you drive to Green Bay in a jeep? Why didn't you use the SEAL?"

"Because you had the keys with you."

The giant chuckled. "No, I didn't. I left them in the transport. Didn't you check before coming after me?"

"No," Yama replied.

"It's my fault," Samson admitted. "I thought the keys were with you."

"Too bad," Blade said. "We could have saved ourselves a lot of trouble if we'd had the SEAL back there. We could have mowed the Automatons down without working up a sweat."

To their surprise, Melissa laughed and shook her head.

"Do you find that funny?" Yama asked.

"In a way, yes," Melissa stated, snickering and giggling.

"How so?"

"It's nice to know that you guys aren't infallible."

Blade looked over his right shoulder at her and grinned. "My wife could have told you that."

AFTER THE NUCLEAR WAR WAS OVER, THE REAL KILLING BEGAN!

They called him Phoenix because he rose from the ashes of destruction. Driven by hatred and thirsting for revenge, he battled nature gone insane and men driven mad by total devastation.

The action/adventure series that's hotter than a thermonuclear explosion!